Unicorns?

F
LAS   Lasky, Kathryn
PB   Unicorns? Get real!

KATHRYN LASKY

Unicorns? Get Real!

A
CAMP PRINCESS
NOVEL

HARPERCOLLINS*PUBLISHERS*

www.harpercollinschildrens.com

Library of Congress Cataloging-in-Publication
Data is available.
ISBN-10: 0-06-058764-4 (trade bdg.)
ISBN-13: 978-0-06-058764-2 (trade bdg.)
ISBN-10: 0-06-058766-0 (pbk. bdg.)
ISBN-13: 978-0-06-058766-6 (pbk. bdg.)

Typography by Sasha Illingworth
1 2 3 4 5 6 7 8 9 10
❖
First Edition

THE PRINCESSES
OF THE SOUTH TURRET

PRINCESS ALICIA QUINTANA MARIELA
MARGARITA

Native country: Belgravia

National flower: The lily

Motto: As strong as it is beautiful: thus
goes the swan

Coat of arms: The coat of arms of the rulers of Belgravia
dates back to the early Middle Ages, when it was said that
the soul of a great warrior fallen in battle returned in the
form of a swan and struck down the enemy leader as he was
about to capture the first child of the king and queen. From
that day hence, the Belgravian swans have always enjoyed
royal protection and are treated as sacred birds.

PRINCESS GUNDERSNAP LUDMILLA
MARIA THERESA

Native country: The Empire of Slobodkonia,
a confederation of Slobodk states ruled by

the Empress Maria Theresa, mother of Gundersnap and fifteen other children

National flower: The prickly thistled cactus. This flower is known to grow only in the rugged highlands of eastern Slobodkonia. Tempting, with gorgeous bright hues ranging from purple to creamy rose, it is impossible to pick without severe injury from the razor-edged leaves and sharp thorns.

Motto: Right rides with might

Coat of arms: The Slobodkonian bull, now extinct. Some believe the bull is reincarnated in the person of the present Empress Maria Theresa, regarded as the most belligerent and aggressive of monarchs because of her fondness for war and invasion.

PRINCESS KRISTINA GUNILLA SOLVYG, CALLED KRISTEN

Native country: The Isles of Salt Tears in the Realm of Rolm

National flower: The ice daisy, a hardy flower that grows exclusively on icebergs in the Realm of Rolm

Motto: Blow, wind, blow: make our salt blood flow

Coat of arms: A sea serpent entwined with the purple whale of Rolm. Centuries ago, this killer whale consumed countless

Rolmian children before it was slain by Bella the Magnificent, the great-great-great-grandmother of Princess Kristen. Previous to that time the coat of arms had merely been a legendary sea serpent of vague origin.

PRINCESS MYRELLA SERENA ASTRIA
Native country: Marsh Kingdoms
National flower: The pink mallow of the marsh
Motto: In mud we trust

Coat of arms: The elegant transformations of marsh creatures such as the frog and the dragonfly are celebrated by the people of the Marsh Kingdoms, who for centuries have embraced their country's swampy and squishy landscape with passion and ingenuity. The frog prince is no mere legend but is based on an inspiring figure of history, a real hero to the citizens of this kingdom. It is said that the first king of the marshes was a certain Gaston de Frogmore who, at one time before his transformation, had indeed been an amphibian of some sort. It was King Frogmore who constructed the first and only stilt palace in the world. The palace still stands on its tall stilt foundations, and its Hall of Reeds is a must-see for every tourist of the region.

Session Two

Dear Royal Camper:

More excitement awaits you at the second session of Camp Princess! In preparation for special second-session activities, these additional items will be required. We suggest ordering them from the special supplement to the *Royal Campers' Equipment Catalogue.*

- One complete riding habit—no hoop skirts permitted, only princess trou!
- Stirrup friendly footwear—no heels, please!
- Crown-jeweled riding helmets with detachable wide sun brims. Helmet must bear the majestic safety seal of approval for protection of royal brains.
- Sleeping bag—with ten-thousand-thread-count lining.

Royal crest or coat of arms must be embroidered on all sleeping bags.

- Water-resistant, sea-serpent-skinned rain garments
- Princess toiletries carry-all. We recommend the Princess-in-a-bag model that comes in a range of colors and with multiple compartments.
- Loom-woven silk mosquito netting (jewel attachments optional)
- Quart-sized sterling silver canteen with royal initials engraved
- Oil of Saint Arachnis insect repellent

Plains of Wesselwick

THE ROYAL CAMPGROUNDS OF
Palacyndra

Lake Alamora

Camp Burning Shield

Greenheart Forest

Camp Princess

Forest of Chimes

"Look, Gilly, at the high heels Princess Alicia is wearing. They got diamonds in them, they do!" a groom from the royal stables whispered in her ear.

"Crispin! What are you doing here?"

"Well, what about yourself?" he replied. The two servants of Camp Princess were hidden in the shadows of a balcony, while below in the ballroom dozens of princesses danced. It was a kaleidoscope of jeweled shoes, jeweled gowns, and gleaming tiaras. They were practicing for the ball next month at Burning Shield, a camp for royal princes across the lake. It would be the first time many of them would dance in high heels and "full pouffiness," which meant wearing two or more crinolines under their ball gowns to make them stick out as far as possible.

Suddenly there were yelps and shrieks.

"Pileup!" Crispin cried out with excitement. More servants raced to the edge of the balcony.

There was the blast of a whistle as Signor Pippinia, the dance master, raced to the center of the ballroom, where a heap of princesses lay sprawled atop one another.

"There's always at least two pileups. It takes the First Years quite a while to get the hang of dancing with the high heels. That's why they always have the Third Years as their partners," Gilly said knowingly to the other servants who stood near her. She was surrounded mostly by scullery girls, laundresses, and stable boys, who knew little of the royal activities, unlike she herself, who had served for several years now as a chambermaid.

"All right, who's taking bets here that it's the Royal Princess Kristen who started this smashup?" a footman said. Footmen were almost as knowledgeable as chambermaids about the princesses. They were in charge of all princesses' transportation, from carriages to horses, and they served princesses at formal occasions—banquets, tournaments, and similar events.

"Oh my goodness!" Gilly moaned. She feared the footman

was right. Princess Kristen from the Realm of Rolm was a wild princess if there ever was one. Charging across the ballroom floor as if she were on the jousting field, Princess Kristen had no use whatsoever for high heels, and she was definitely not accustomed to crinolines and full pouffiness. Leather jerkins, high boots, and wide-cut britches were her favorite clothing. She had protested mightily the entire time Gilly and another chambermaid were dressing her in the layers of crinolines. "Worse than a pony with a burr under its saddle," Gilly had muttered, to which Kristen had replied, "I'd much prefer a burr to being smothered in all this."

Next they had attempted to teach her to walk in the high heels. But she balked at even taking a single step. "Stubborn as a royal mule, she is!" Gilly again muttered. First a pony and then a mule! Yes, Princess Kristen was the wild one of the group. Wild as any animal.

When the princesses had arrived at camp for the first session, Gilly had prayed that the ones of South Turret, where she served, would not be snotty as the princesses from the previous summer. Well, the princesses were not snotty. They were as nice as could be. But they were also very independent-minded. Gilly knew for a fact that they often sneaked out at night. But she was no tattletale, and they didn't seem any the worse for it. So why worry?

In addition to the wild Princess Kristen, the South Turret was home to Princess Alicia of All the Belgravias—a real beauty, if there ever was one. Charming, delicate, but strong-willed in her own way. Then dear, squat Princess Gundersnap of the Empire of Slobodkonia, a war-inclined nation ruled by her fierce mother, the Empress Maria Theresa. Now there was an interesting princess. In all her years of being a chamber-maid, Gilly had never had a princess like her. Gundersnap displayed not the slightest twinge of homesickness. And she constantly had to be reminded to write home.

New to the South Turret this session was tiny Princess Myrella of the Marsh Kingdoms. In the previous session, the princess had had the unfortunate experience of turreting with two of the meanest princesses in the camp: Princess Morwenna and Princess Millicent. Alicia, Kristen, and Gundersnap had become good friends with Myrella and wrote to the Camp Mistress formally requesting, indeed begging, for Myrella to be transferred to their turret for this session. She was so tiny, and there was plenty of room, they argued. So it was arranged. Princess Myrella moved out of the North Turret, where she was replaced by Princess Zelenka, also quite nasty, who fit perfectly with the other two.

Myrella was so happy to get out of the North Turret, she said she did not mind sleeping in the wardrobe closet at all, so it had been very plushly outfitted for her. There was a bureau in the closet with exceptionally large drawers. The royal carpenter had been summoned and had fashioned the top drawer into a lovely little bed for the tiny princess. The middle drawer had been turned upside down and served as a desktop, and the one below that had been lined with cushions for Myrella to sit in. Myrella called these lower drawers her "study" and found this vertical living arrangement quite to her liking.

Gilly peered over the edge of the balcony and watched Gundersnap as she straightened out her tiara, muttering in the strange language known as Slobo.

Signor Pippinia was now addressing the princesses.

"Dancing is an art form, my ladies. It is not a race, Princess Kristen. And now that you are having your first try with high heels, we need to think control and balance. So we are having slow dances. Let me demonstrate." He snapped his fingers. A servant came forward with a pillow. Perched on the pillow was a pair of high-heeled red velvet shoes with emeralds embedded in the heels. Signor Pippinia slipped off his boots. "Luckily the Queen Mum and I are the same size. She has kindly lent me her shoes, which are perfect for my high-heeled demonstration." He nodded at Queen Mother Adelia Elsinore Louisa, the Camp Mistress. "Now observe." He clicked his fingers, and the musicians began to play a slow tune with a heavy beat. "One-two-three and one-two-three . . . a nice little dip and then a twirl and then one-two-three and one-two-three." He swirled by the Princess Gundersnap and bowed to her. She took his hand. The smoothness went out of Signor Pippinia's step, and it became more of a march.

Gilly rolled her eyes.

"Easy, easy, Princess Gundersnap," the dance master cautioned. "We are not on a battlefield with your mother the empress, thank goodness. We are in a ballroom. You want to lead? Oh sure, no problem."

Princess Gundersnap got a glint in her eye. Sticking her neck forward, she began to shove the dance master around the ballroom floor. *He might as well be a battering ram,* Gilly thought. And then again wondered, as she had so many times, how come she had been born a simple servant and these girls royal princesses, born to rule. She just knew that she would be a much more graceful dancer than any one of them.

Oops! Gundersnap had just plowed into another pair of dancers, who went on a wild skid across the ballroom. Four jeweled high-heeled shoes flew up into the air.

"Got it!" Crispin yelled as he reached over the balcony and caught a pearl-encrusted shoe that had flown in a lofty arc toward the ceiling.

Chapter 1

GUNDERSNAP'S PROCLAMATION

Princess Gundersnap sat down at the desk in her chamber and took a piece of paper and a quill pen. She chewed the end of the quill. Within a minute the end was in shreds. "Oh dear!" She sighed. "What can I write Mummy?" Maria Theresa, Empress of All the Slobodks, was not your warm and cuddly kind of mum. Gundersnap sighed once more and dipped the pen into the inkwell.

> *Dear Empress Mummy, Royal Majesty of the*
> *Empire of Slobodkonia,*
> *It is not quite summer as it should be. But that*

often happens here at Camp Princess with its odd seasons. At least it's not winter. Let's say it's autumn in July. Although I am happy to be here, I of course will miss terribly our usual summer sojourns to the Convent of the Sisters of Perpetual Misery. I'll miss our lovely hours together kneeling on the stone floors while praying for your successful invasions of a kingdom. This year it is to be the Empire of Hottompot, is it not? How excited my dear sister Princess Zelda must be that you may capture a prince for her there!

"And how lucky I am to be the ninth daughter!" murmured Gundersnap. There were at least four more daughters ahead of her who would have to be married off, not counting sons. Maybe there would be a shortage of kingdoms to invade when her turn came to be married. Maybe the supply of eligible princes would have dried up and she could actually marry someone of her own choosing. Although she doubted the supply would run dry anytime soon. Across the lake at Camp Burning Shield, there seemed to be plenty of royal princes. Alicia, her turretmate, who was more than slightly boy crazy, was constantly asking when the dance with Burning Shield would be. Gundersnap continued writing.

I want to thank you for allowing Gortle to come to camp for this session. I cannot wait until he arrives. I am sure he will entertain us well.

"Fat Chance!" Gundersnap muttered. If there was one thing that Princess Gundersnap snapped over, it was the ill treatment of court dwarves. The poor little humans suffered various painful conditions and health problems that ranged from backaches to terrible headaches. Yet they were supposed to be constantly tumbling, juggling, and performing tricks for the court. "Positively nauseating!" Gundersnap hissed.

Once campers had been in camp for one session, they were permitted to bring a servant to provide light entertainment—a family court jester, a juggler, a tumbler, or a troubadour. Gundersnap, however, was not bringing Gortle as a source of light entertainment, but to free him from what she considered the abuses of court life in Slobodkonia. Her mother, however, didn't need to know that. She continued:

Well, I must close now as it is time for my evening prayers. My thoughts are with you on this campaign. Please give my love to all fifteen

of my dear brothers and sisters. And—she looked up at the painting over her desk of her dear pony—*a hug for Menschmik, and do give him one of those golden apples that he so loves.*
Yours Very Truly,
Royal Princess Gundersnap Ludmilla Maria Theresa of the Empire of Slobodkonia

As she finished the letter, Princess Gundersnap could hear the voices of her turretmates in the main salon. She crept toward the door to listen.

"Holy monk bones! What in the name of Saint Sammy is this?" she heard Princess Alicia saying.

Then Princess Kristen began reading aloud the note Gundersnap had left on the salon table.

Let it be understood that Gortle Zurf, court dwarf from the Empire of Slobodkonia, arrives in a few days and will not be here for my or anyone else's entertainment. I deplore the use of extremely short human beings as a source of amusement. I am bringing him here expressly to spare him such abuses. He is here as my dear friend and confidant. Please attend to the following regulations: And I mean it. Smurchdot!

(That means "Listen up" in Slobo.)

He shall not be asked to tumble.

He shall not be asked to jump through hoops.

He shall not be asked to ride aboard a dog or any creature other than a pony or horse of appropriate size.

He shall not be asked to sing, talk in a funny voice, or tell jokes.

He shall be treated with all the courtesy and respect that is extended to full-size adult human beings.

These regulations are issued by me, the Royal Princess Gundersnap of the Empire of Slobodkonia.

Princess Kristen finished reading the document. There was silence for several seconds, and then Gundersnap could hear Princess Myrella's voice.

"I think she's right," said the tiny princess of the Marsh Kingdoms. "My own family hasn't kept dwarves for years."

"We never kept dwarves," said Kristen. "The Realm of Rolm is simply too cold for them. They'd get terrible arthritis."

"Besides, dwarves are so ⁄ . . so twelfth century," said

Princess Alicia. "Troubadours, your ordinary court jester—that's one thing—but dwarves—that is so over!"

"Indeed!" said a new voice. It belonged to Lady Merry von Schleppenspiel, the princesses' lady-in-waiting. She was an immensely large lady with cascading multiple chins. She preferred the words "large" or "ample" to "fat." "You know Gundersnap is a sensitive girl. She worries about everyone except herself," said Lady Merry with a sigh.

Gundersnap coughed loudly to give warning and then came through the door. "Dearie," Lady Merry said, "we completely agree with you about Gortle. He should come for afternoon tea when he arrives. We'll have a nice game of whist. He shall be entertained and not be the entertainment!" She nodded, and all eight of her chins trembled in fleshy agreement.

At just that moment, there was the loud tinkling of a bell. "Enter," Lady Merry sang out.

Four chambermaids came in to the salon, each carrying a freshly ironed nightgown. And one also carried a scroll listing the next few days' activities.

Gilly, Alicia's personal chambermaid and really the favorite of them all, stepped forward, smiling brightly. "You'll be glad to hear that if the weather is good, there is to be no makeup class tomorrow with the Duchess of Bagglesnort."

There was a resounding "hooray" from all four princesses. The Snort, as they called the duchess, was their least favorite counselor. "No, Miladies, something much better."

"Vot is it?" When Princess Gundersnap became excited, she often lapsed into her heavy Slobodkonian accent, in which "w" became "v."

"Unicorns!" Gilly replied.

Princess Gundersnap gasped. She could hardly believe it. Hadn't she thought she had seen the dim outline of such a creature in the unfinished tapestry last session? One of the great mysteries of the castle, which only the princesses of the South Turret knew about, was the magical tapestry in a hidden turret. During that first session of camp, Alicia had been led there by a Ghost Princess who had haunted her bedchamber. The ghost had told Alicia that her spirit could only be put to rest if the three princesses of the South Turret completed the part of the tapestry that had never been finished. Alicia, Gundersnap, and Kristen had begun to sew, and it was as if their hands had been magically guided, for as they stitched a picture began to emerge. Not an entire picture, but one with enough clues so that eventually the spirit of the Ghost Princess and that of her true love, a knight, could be reunited and put to rest.

Gundersnap could remember it all as clearly as if it had happened five minutes ago. Just as Princess Alicia had said, "I guess the tapestry is finished. The story told," Gundersnap had seen some other lines that were ever so faint. At first she thought it was the figure of a small horse, but the harder she looked, the more it had seemed like a unicorn. Gundersnap, however, being Gundersnap, was a very practical girl, and she knew that unicorns were just made-up creatures from fairy tales. Her mother had said such creatures didn't exist! And if her mother said something . . . well . . . the empress was usually right about everything. Gundersnap had never said a word to Alicia or Kristen about what she thought she had seen. And Princess Myrella did not even know yet about the unfinished tapestry, for she had not been their turretmate then.

But right now Gilly was saying that in the Kingdom of Palacyndra, there had once been many herds of unicorns. "You see, Miladies, unicorn roundups used to be the most popular activity at Camp Princess, but the herds thinned because we've had so many frequent and severe winters. The remaining herds migrated far south. There has not been a roundup in the years I've been here. But they might be back!"

Kristen was about to jump out of her kirtle from excitement. But Gundersnap was simply astonished. *I wonder,*

Gundersnap thought, *if they really do exist, if they are magi-cal too, like the ones in fairy tales? Ach, never!*

"By Saint Guy, this is exciting!" Kristen was exclaiming.

"Guy? Guys?" said Alicia vaguely. "Guys like boys?"

"No, like Guy of Anderlet, patron saint of horses and things with horns. It's so totally ice."

"Totally ice" was one of Kristen's favorite expressions. The people of the Realm of Rolm, where it was very cold, had many odd expressions that involved ice, snow, and harsh weather, which the inhabitants seemed to love and find bracing. "Totally ice" was one of those expressions especially popular among the younger generation in the realm.

Kristen turned to Gilly. "Will there be a real roundup where we go out and sleep in tents and follow the herds?"

"Maybe." Gilly smiled. "Weather permitting, that is. But in the meantime, in arts and crafts you shall be making satin ribbon lanyards in preparation. These will be your lariats for lassoing unicorns."

"Great!" said Princess Kristen. "I am so darned sick of making those stupid diamond barrettes!"

"So to bed with you all." Lady Merry was waving them toward their chambers and Myrella toward her closet. "If you are to go on unicorn roundup, you will need all your energy." She continued, "For you shall be riding for hours all day over the plains of Wesselwick. Sleeping in tents, eating camp food. Very tiring. And none of this breakfast in bed stuff."

"Uh-oh!" said Princess Alicia.

"Yes, yes, Princess Alicia. You'll have to toughen up." Lady Merry shook one of her plump beringed fingers at the princess.

"My *mudder*, the empress, goes to battle," Gundersnap added. "No breakfast in bed, and she eats the same food as her soldiers. She always says, '*Schlobenspuk besmutch da besmutch schlobenspuk.*'"

"Can you translate that, Gunny?" Alicia asked.

"Yes, it means 'When the going gets tough, the tough get going.'"

Each princess bade the others good night. In the princesses' bedchambers, the chambermaids got busy. First they sprayed a lovely night scent of perfume about. It was called Sweet Royal Dreams. They lit reading candles and arranged small mountains of lace pillows—except in Kristen's bedchamber, since she preferred plain cotton ones edged with canvas ruffles. They reminded her of her favorite sailing vessel, the *Glory Be*, in which she had won the junior division of the Realm of Rolm Regatta. After the chambermaids had unhooked an average of one hundred and thirty-two hooks, unbuttoned seventy-five buttons of the princesses' gowns, and unlaced at least twenty feet of strings and ribbons that held up various petticoats and under-petticoats, their royal charges were at last ready for bed.

Princess Kristen now clasped her hands in prayer as she knelt by her bed. "Oh please, dear Lord, and Saint Guy of Anderlet, may the weather be permitting, and may we get to go on the roundup."

"What about Camp Burning Shield, dear Lord?" Princess Alicia prayed. "Any chance they might be going on the roundup? Oh please please please! We haven't even had a dance with Camp Burning Shield yet! So a roundup would be nice. Amen. Oh, P.S., bless Mum and Pops and my dear sisters Lorelei and Isabella. Oh yes, Isabella has pinkeye and poison ivy—royal bummer! Make it go away. Love and kisses, and don't forget about Camp Burning Shield. Amen again."

Princess Myrella dropped to her knees and asked the Lord for nothing, but only thanked him over and over for answering her prayers that she could live with Alicia, Gundersnap, and Kristen, and finally be out of the North Turret and away from the awful Princess Morwenna and Princess Millicent. They were not only the meanest princesses in the entire camp, but they cheated as well—

always up to dirty tricks in every camp competition. "Thank you, thank you, Lord, thank you so much for delivering me from those vile, horrible girls and letting me join this turret with the very best and kindest princesses of the whole camp."

Princess Gundersnap furrowed her brow and then, kneeling, began her prayer.

"Dear Lord, bless Empress Mummy and the rest of the lot. I don't have time to go through all the fifteen names of my brothers and sisters—or is it sixteen now, did Mudder have another—well I'm sure you know who I mean by now, and please please please bless my dear pony Menschmik."

And then Princess Gundersnap prayed that dear Gortle's arrival not be delayed because of the crazy weather in Palacyndra.

Chapter 2

THE AGONY OF PRINCESS GUNDERSNAP

There would be no roundup or unicorn activities yet, because outside a blizzard raged. It had begun suddenly, in the middle of the night, as storms so often do in Palacyndra. But in the Princess Parlor, there was a large roaring fire and the princesses were toasting marshmallows, then putting the melted marshmallow between two biscuits with a chunk of chocolate. These special treats were called s'moroyals, or s'morls for short. So despite the blizzard, everything in the parlor was cozy, and all the princesses cheerful as could be. Except, that is, for Gundersnap, who sat in the window seat looking mournfully out the window, eating s'morls and wondering if Gortle would ever make it through the snow-drifts. "Now come on, Gundersnap," Alicia urged. "Listen to this!" Princess Alicia sat curled up in a plush winged chair reading the latest issue of *The Royal We*.

The Royal We was a gossip magazine that specialized in tittle-tattle of the major kingdoms' courts. "Listen to this and take your mind off Gortle for a minute. You're going to make yourself sick with all those, by the way."

"Vot is it?" asked Gundersnap, stopping mid bite. It was her twelfth s'morl of the morning. Alicia held up the magazine. There was a portrait of King Harry of Britmoria and a glamorous-looking woman laden in diamonds. The words shrieked from the page "HARRY AND QUEEN TO SPLIT!"

"The man has had five wives already. What's his problem?" asked Princess Kinna of the Queendom of Mattunga—a tall, slender princess with skin the color of cinnamon.

Gundersnap was out of her chair immediately. "*Gunshuch mygott!* My *mudder* was going to marry off my sister Brunhilda to him. But he thought she wasn't pretty enough and instead took this woman—a commoner, but quite beautiful. Vot happened?"

"She's a witch!" Princess Zelenka said.

"Get out!" Alicia said disdainfully. "You haven't even read the story. It says here, and I quote, 'Vivacious court beauty Katrina Beaufort is said to have caught the notoriously roving eye of King Harry. Katrina, a tireless dancer as well as a tireless flirt—see box on her simultaneous romances with the Duke of Bottomsley and the Prince of Argylle—when asked about her romance with His Majesty, replied, "No comment." Will the fetching Katrina be the sixth Mrs. H.?'"

In the midst of Alicia's reading, the parlor door was flung open and a small, rugged man came whirling in like a high-speed snowball.

"Gortle!" Gundersnap yelped, then jumped up and ran toward the dwarf. She bent over to hug him fiercely. She hoped that the other princesses saw that she *did not* pick him up. People were always picking up dwarves as if they were toddlers and tossing them about. Her mother the empress loved scooping up the small man and bouncing him about as if he were a large rubber ball. But he was a man, not a toy.

"Oh Gortle! Gortle! I am so glad you made it through the blizzard."

"Strange weather for late July, I do say," he replied, brushing snow from his cape. He removed a funny little cap with earflaps to reveal a thick mass of deep rusty-red curls. His mustache swooped up in twists on either side of a broad nose that reminded Gundersnap of a breakfast bun. He was short, the top of his head not an inch above Gundersnap's waist.

"Oh, that's Palacyndra for you," Kristen said.

"Oh Gortle." Gundersnap turned toward Kristen. "These are my turretmates, Princess Kristen, Princess Alicia, and Princess Myrella."

"Heard all about you, Princesses," he said with a merry glint in his bright blue eyes. Kristen shook his hand, bending over slightly in just the manner Gundersnap had instructed them to use when greeting a dwarf. But Myrella, who was just his size, perhaps an inch or so taller, walked up and gave him a firm handshake, looking him straight in the eye.

"So pleased to make your acquaintance." She heard Princesses Zelenka and Millicent snicker. Gundersnap shot them an absolutely poisonous glance.

"Any news from Mummy and the invasion? Hottompot, isn't it?" Gundersnap asked.

A fleeting shadow crossed Gortle's face. "Oh, I've brought a letter, but plenty of time to read that later," the dwarf replied.

"Come have a s'morl," Alicia offered.

At just that moment, Princesses Zelenka, Millicent, and Morwenna approached. Myrella got a dreadful feeling in her tummy as she saw her old turretmates. *Here comes royal trouble*, she thought to herself.

Millicent stooped down in a crouch. "Tell me, little man, do you tumble?"

"Uh-oh!" Alicia, Myrella, and Kristen all said at once.

Gundersnap was on the Princess Millicent like a cat pouncing on a mouse. And the only tumbling to be seen was a swirl of petticoats and flying tiaras as the two princesses rolled across the parlor floor. When they stopped, Gundersnap leaped to her feet and dragged up the stunned Princess Millicent by her frothy lace collar. "His name is Gortle Zurf, not 'little man,' you royal nincompoop. He does not tumble. He does not talk in a funny voice. Nor does he ride a dog for your entertainment, or jump through hoops. He is an adult and my friend. He is here for my companionship and not as entertainment for you. Got that, Princess?" Gundersnap rapped her knuckles on Princess Millicent's head.

"Yes, yes, of course."

"I've never heard of a dwarf that didn't tumble," Princess Morwenna said.

"And I've never heard of a pious princess who cheats in Color Wars!" Gundersnap roared at the dour Morwenna. A titter mixed with gasps surged through the Princess Parlor.

"That's a direct hit!" Kristen whispered.

Indeed it was, for in last session's canoeing race it had been none other than the excessively pious and constantly prayerful Princess Morwenna and Princess Zelenka who had tried to sideswipe the Purple team, nearly forcing them onto the rocks. Those cheating Crimsons!

Gortle conducted himself with perfect calm, not even seeming to notice Princess Morwenna's rude behavior. For her part, Princess Gundersnap set about to correct anybody's notions of Gortle as a source of dwarfish entertainment. First she played chess with him. This was followed by a performance of Gundersnap's songbird, whom she had taught to sing and march to a rousing Slobodkonian tune called "The March of the Fifth Artillery."

"Your mum the empress would be so pleased," said Gortle. Then there were more s'morls and a tour of the castle. Gortle was entertained royally and *not* the royal entertainment.

It wasn't until after dinner, when the four princesses were cozy in their own parlor in the South Turret, that Gundersnap remembered to ask for the letter. Gortle looked up nervously from the card game he was playing with Lady Merry.

"Oh yes, nearly forgot." He reached into his vest and drew

out an envelope with the royal seal of the Empress Maria Theresa of Slobodkonia. Gundersnap began to open it.

"Uh . . . Your Highness."

Gundersnap now saw for the first time the worry on his face.

"Maybe you should read this in privacy."

A silence fell over the turret parlor. The envelope began to tremble in Gundersnap's hand. "What is it?" she said in barely a whisper. Gortle shook his head, but no words would come out.

Gundersnap rushed into her bedchamber to read the letter. *What could it be?* she wondered. *A battle lost? A baby sister or brother had died?* Her hands were shaking so hard now that she could barely make out her mother's bold handwriting. There was a scream. Then . . .

"She didn't! NO! NO! NO!" In the parlor the princesses looked at one another in horror. The words were clear, but the sound Gundersnap made was like an animal caught in a trap.

"What is it?" Kristen asked.

"Her mother, the empress,"—Gortle nearly spat out the words, so great was his contempt—"she has taken Gundersnap's favorite pony into battle. She has made him a war pony."

"Menschmick!" Alicia cried. They had all heard about dear little Menschmick practically from the hour Gundersnap first arrived at Camp Princess.

Gortle nodded and sighed wearily. "They are quick-moving little fellows in close combat. But ponies never last long in battle. Their hearts give out. They aren't made for war."

Princess Gundersnap was now sobbing hysterically. The three princesses and Gortle ran into her bedchamber to comfort her.

Princess Gundersnap had collapsed facedown on her bed. The letter was on the floor beside her. "He was my birthday present! How could she have done that? My little Menschmik in battle! The thought is too horrible." She beat her fists into the pillow. And when she finally lifted her head, the princesses were shocked. Gundersnap's plump face looked ravaged. Tears streamed from her tiny, sad eyes.

Lady Merry had finally hoisted herself out of her chair and waddled in. "Princess! Princess! Yes, it is a terrible thing your mother, the empress, has done." She wanted to say that the empress was not worth it, but stopped herself. Instead she said, "But don't make yourself sick over it."

As if in answer, Princess Gundersnap's face turned a sudden and rather noxious shade of green. There was a throaty gulp and then a splat as Gundersnap threw up the even dozen s'morls she had eaten that morning. It all landed right on the letter.

"Oh ick!" said Kristen.

Gundersnap looked down at the mess and blinked. *"Ingen Gutschatz mychenbatuz schumckenhaben Mummy,"* which roughly translated from Slobo meant, "I wish it was on Mummy's head!"

Chapter 3

GUNDERSNAP'S BRIGHT IDEA

The next morning Princesses Myrella, Kristen, and Alicia were excused from needlepoint so they could visit Gundersnap in the infirmary. Kristen had a vial of tummy powders from Gortle tucked beneath her kirtle, along with a note for Gundersnap.

"It works, miladies," Gortle had said to them after he gave the vial to Kristen. "Lady Merry tells me that old Nurse Bodkin hasn't moved out of the thirteenth century with her cures. I remember Gundersnap writing me about some horrible remedy Bodkin had for a sinus condition."

"Held open the beak of a live sparrow and made you

stick your nose in it," Alicia said. "Absolutely horrid, and the sparrow had bad breath!"

This prompted Kristen to recount for at least the fifth time the story of how she had cut her foot swimming and the old biddy Bodkin was set to do the maggot therapy on her. "Said it would prevent a scar. I said, who's going to look at the bottom of my foot anyhow? I'd rather have a scar than a bunch of maggots eating at a banquet table that just happens to be my foot."

The infirmary was empty, but on one side of the room a door with the words "Medicinal Menagerie" painted on it in gold was slightly open. The room behind the door gave them the absolute creeps, but they could not resist a peek. From where they stood, they could see jars filled with all sorts of disgusting things. One held a writhing mass of maggots. Another contained a murky liquid floating with leeches. On a table a small population of toads hopped about in a terrarium. A label on its side read "Nurse Bodkin's Special Spotted Toads for Treatment of Warts." A second terrarium was asquirm with lizards.

The girls jumped back as the door swung wide open and Nurse Bodkin came out with a large bird perched on her arm. She was a strange-looking woman. Her complexion was sallow, and her skin crackled like an old manuscript.

Her nose, however, was a vivid purple, with a tracery of minuscule blood vessels that reminded the princesses of exploding fireworks.

"Good grief, it's that stupid caladrius bird, Rufus," muttered Princess Kristen.

"What's that?" asked Myrella.

"I was just about to administer the CBDE on your friend Princess Gundersnap, dear." Nurse Bodkin said.

"The C-B what?" Alicia asked.

"The Caladrius Bird Diagnostic Evaluation. We did it with your foot, Kristen, to determine if you were going to die of blood poisoning. Very accurate."

"Accurate, my foot!" Kristen said in a low, sarcastic voice. "I could have told her that without the bird."

"As a matter of fact, Your Highnesses, would you mind taking Rufus to Princess Gundersnap's bed. I'll be there in a moment, but I have to go lance a boil."

"Oh, don't worry about it, Nurse Bodkin," Princess Alicia said. "We'll take care of everything."

Princess Kristen stuck out her arm, and the bird stepped onto it.

Before she even greeted Gundersnap, Princess Kristen walked to the window, opened it, and stuck her arm out. "Scram, you quack! It's only modern medicine here. Go find a real job." The bird blinked at her as if he didn't quite believe what she was saying was true. Then it spread its wings and flew off.

Alicia giggled. "Kristen, you'll get in trouble."

"I'll think of something."

"What is it with the bird, anyhow? If the caladrius looks at you, you'll live. If it looks away, you die?" Alicia asked.

"Something like that," Kristen said, and turned to Gundersnap. "But how are you feeling, Gunny? Gortle sent some tummy powders."

Princess Gundersnap just sighed. "I must be practical. There is absolutely nothing I can do about this. So I must clear it from my mind and not vorry, I mean worry." Still, there was a sadness in Gundersnap's eyes that touched them all. She held in her hands a little leather pouch.

"What's that?" Alicia asked.

Gundersnap's eyes filled with tears. "Gortle gave it to me with the letter. It's strands from Menschmik's mane. They always cut a pony's mane when it goes into battle. It . . . it's not practical!" She shut her eyes very tightly, as if to will away her tears. When she opened them again, there was a new brightness.

"I have just had an idea." She paused. "I mean, it's more than just an idea. You know the problem with Menschmik seems hopeless, doesn't it?" She looked at the three princesses with mournful eyes. "Admit it, it does." Alicia, Myrella, and Kristen nodded their heads softly.

"Yes, I suppose so," Myrella said in barely a whisper.

"But," Gundersnap said, suddenly chipper, "Myrella doesn't know about Berwynna."

"Ber-who?" Myrella asked.

"Berwynna! I must go to the Forest of Chimes and find her. If anyone can help me, it's Berwynna."

"What a brilliant idea!" Alicia exclaimed. She turned to Myrella, who knew nothing of Berwynna or the unfinished tapestry or the Ghost Princess that Alicia and Kristen and Gundersnap had encountered the last session. "I was the first to discover Berwynna," Alicia said. "She is a little old lady, and a very strange one at that. She lives in the Forest of Chimes. It is said that she is Merlin the magician's sister. Her magic isn't half as good or half as strong, and sometimes she messes up a little bit. But she gave us hints about the unfinished tapestry, which was really the key to it all," Alicia said. "I mean, the key to the Ghost Princess and why my bird finally did sing."

"Why yes, it sang brilliantly," Myrella said, bewildered. "You won the Color Wars for us with his song. No cheating. But a Ghost Princess?"

"No cheating at all, even though magic was involved," Alicia said firmly. "You see, the unfinished tapestry was almost like a crystal ball. It told us things—not every little thing, but it gave hints." Alicia sighed. "But it's finished now. There is nothing else to tell."

Gundersnap cast her eyes down. She had not told them about the dim traces of the unicorn—that indeed the tapestry might still be unfinished. She had more important things to think about. *This isn't about the tapestry*, she told herself. *Not at all. And certainly not about unicorns!*

"The tapestry is finished," Gundersnap said firmly, "but that doesn't mean Berwynna can't help. She's the only one who can help me, really. Help Menschmik." Gundersnap's voice broke again, and tears brimmed in her eyes.

"But how did you first meet her, Alicia?" Myrella asked.

"Well, you see," Alicia began slowly. "You remember when I was castled?"

"How could anyone forget?" Myrella said. Alicia had been castled for being rude to the Duchess of Bagglesnort. Being castled meant that Alicia could not leave the confines of not just the castle, but the South Turret. "I wasn't quite as 'castled' as one might think. The very day I was castled, I snuck out into the Forest of Chimes, and that's when I met her."

"You did?" Myrella said. She could not believe how daring these princesses were. Oh, how much fun she would have this session. "When can we go to the Forest of Chimes?"

"I must go alone first," Gundersnap said. "This is my problem, but when I learn more . . ."

Just then Nurse Bodkin poked her head in. "Ready for the CBDE? My dear?"

"Oh dear, Nurse Bodkin. I'm afraid the Rufus flew out the window. It was open slightly," Alicia said, crossing her fingers.

"Oh . . . oh . . ." Nurse Bodkin's pale-gray eyes darted around the chamber in confusion. "Well, he'll come back, I'm sure. They always do. I'll get the backup bird."

"Oh, no need," Gundersnap said quickly. "I feel fine. My tummy's fine."

"My, what a remarkable recovery!" Nurse Bodkin said. "But you should still eat lightly, Your Highness, for the next twenty-four hours: calf's-foot jelly, no greasy meat, avoid rich desserts, and s'morls are out!"

"Oh yes, Nurse. Never another s'morl, never."

Chapter 4

BIDING ROYAL TIME

Nurse Bodkin continued to call out instructions to the princesses as they hurried down the long corridor, but they were planning how they could sneak off to the hidden turret to have another look at the tapestry while Gundersnap went to the Forest of Chimes.

"Miladies! Makeup, cosmetics! You're late. The duchess is waiting." A maid stopped them.

"Oh, dung of a pig!" exclaimed Kristen.

"Tell the Snort that I'm still too sick to come. I have to go *now*."

"It's still winter, though," Myrella said.

"Alicia, can I borrow your bear-paw model snowshoes?" Gundersnap asked.

"Oh, lucky you!" Kristen said. "I've been trying to borrow them forever."

"This is a life-or-death situation, Kristen." Alicia immediately regretted her words as she saw Gundersnap turn pale. "I mean . . . I mean . . . it's just very important that Gundersnap get to the Forest of Chimes as quickly as possible. They're under my bed, Gundersnap, by the stack of old *Royal We*'s."

"All right, I'm off! Have fun in makeup!"

"Oh yes, of course, makeup! About as much fun as a romp on the torture chamber rack," Kristen muttered.

Along with half a dozen other princesses, Alicia, Myrella, and Kristen filed into the Salon de Beauté. Over the door hung a needlepoint banner that showed the face of the Duchess of Bagglesnort herself in full cosmetic glory. She wore every adornment and trick, from an enticing beauty spot near the corner of her mouth to a head full of braids and ringlets artfully attached to her own hair. Stitched at the bottom of the banner were the words "Adornment is a Duty, Not an Indulgence."

The Duchess of Bagglesnort was full of such sayings and was constantly referring to what she so cutely called "the beauty duty." And she always began each class with a little beauty proverb or epigram. Now she tapped a mascara wand for attention. "Princesses, welcome to the Salon de Beauté. I should like to begin with a wise and very profound saying by one of the great beauties of all times." She smiled sweetly and tried to blush. "Me. And here are my first words of advice: Trickery in service to beauty is honorable."

"In other words, cheat!" Kristen whispered.

"And I have devised a new trick to serve our needs." Her eyes scanned the room. "Now where is that drab little Slobodk princess?"

"Recovering, ma'am," Alicia said. "She's had a terrible bout of tummy troubles."

"Oh dear, I hope they didn't make her look any pastier than she already is," the duchess said in a disgustingly sweet voice.

Kristen rolled her eyes.

"What are you rolling your eyes about, Princess Kristen? It is not an attractive gesture, particularly for a flame child." The Snort referred to Kristen as a flame child because of her vivid coloring and intensely red hair. She rapped on the table again with her mascara wand. "Now attention. We have a new hair exercise. Blondes on this side, and others over here, and oh dear, where to put our flame children?"

She looked at Princess Maggie of Schottlandia, whose hair was even redder than Kristen's.

Then she walked over to Kristen and lifted one of her tresses. "Hmmm." She pressed her lips together and studied the hair.

"I'm an other, aren't I, ma'am, and so is Maggie?"

"No," the duchess said sharply. "You and Maggie are in a category all by yourselves. Stand over there, the two of you." She rang a bell. Fifteen maids with baskets filed into the room. "These are the new attendants of the *coiffeuse*, the hair maids. They bring with them baskets of additional hair—braids, curls, and cascades. We shall begin by attempting to attain a perfect match between the hair that grows out of your scalp and the hairpieces in the basket." She paused, then looked from Kristen and Maggie to the woman who appeared to be the chief attendant of the *coiffeuse*. "Flame children." She nodded toward Kristen and Maggie. "Always a problem. They flare!"

"No problem, ma'am," Kristen said. "I've never taken much to fake hair."

The Duchess of Bagglesnort's eyes nearly popped out of her head. "You think this is artificial hair? I would never put a strand of those terrible wooly hairpieces on my head or the head of a princess!" She turned to the hair maids. "Hair maids, remove your mobcaps." In unison the maids pulled off their puffy white caps. The princesses all gasped in disbelief.

"Bald!" exclaimed Alicia.

"Chaume!" whispered Princess Parisiana in Chantillip.

"Skallet!" croaked a princess from the distant north.

"Schuben!" said another princess.

"Gragg!" Kristen said in the ancient language of the Isles of the Salt Tear in the Realm of Rolm.

"Yes," trilled the Duchess of Bagglesnort. "They are all bald, bald as billiard balls!" She ran her hand over one of the hair maid's shiny scalps. "We pay them a good price. Twenty schmilders an inch. We harvested at the end of last session. Then they will grow it out for the rest of the year."

Twenty schmilders! Alicia thought. *Twenty schmilders is nothing. And their poor heads must get cold.*

There was a sharp little cry and then a thud as Princess Beba, a new camper, collapsed on the floor in a swoon. She had been standing with the blondes, her own luxuriant hair spilling in cascades down her back. "No one ever cuts their hair in the Kingdom of Marlont," someone whispered.

"Yes, to have short hair is considered uncivilized."

"Loutish."

"It's like going naked in public."

"Pay attention! Pay attention. The footmen will remove her," the duchess said, stepping over the fallen princess. Princess Beba was gone less than ten minutes while the duchess explained the intricacies of blending the various shades of hair.

When the princess came back into the Salon de Beauté, she walked unsteadily.

"She's transparent!" Alicia said in a hushed voice.

"Well, it was such a shock," someone else said.

"Dead, she looks totally dead," Kristen said.

"Totally!" Myrella echoed.

"Gorgeous!" the Snort exclaimed, and rushed to Princess Beba. "Simply gorgeous. Now, Miladies, this is just the pallor we try to attain with our powders and clay. It is the classic swoon pallor—white with a hint of ash!" Princess Beba swayed a bit, and her eyes opened wide. Was she going to faint again? There was a sudden gagging noise, and then from the princess's mouth something jetted out in a great gush.

"Holy monk bones!" Alicia exclaimed.

"She spewed!" said Princess Kinna.

"She threw up!" said Myrella.

"She barfed," said Kristen.

"Gutsfop," said the princess from the far north.

The duchess's face was not the classic pallor, but was covered in an olive green slime. A look of sheer terror filled her eyes. She gave a little yelp and then collapsed on the floor.

Kristen stepped over the limp body and snapped her fingers. "Footman! Will you kindly remove the Duchess of Bagglesnort."

"Princess Beba, by the wits of Saint Janny! Your color has returned," Alicia exclaimed.

"Saint Janny? Who's she?" Princess Beba asked.

"It's not a she. It's a he. Saint Januarius, patron saint of blood. You see, Princess Beba. . . ." Alicia began to speak. She was known for her fascination with saints, particularly the gory details of their deaths and martyrdoms. "His blood was preserved and dried, and on his feast day it is said that the dried blood liquefies."

"You don't say!" Princess Beba replied. She seemed suddenly quite perky. The other princesses pressed closer now to hear every gruesome little detail.

"Have you ever seen the dried blood liquefy, Princess Alicia?" Beba asked.

"I have!" a voice from the rear of the Salon de Beauté spoke up.

"Wouldn't you know it!" whispered Myrella.

It was Princess Morwenna, that unsettling and obnoxious mix of piety and spite. She made her way up to the front of the salon. Placing her hand lightly on her chest as if counting the beats of her reverent heart, she arranged her face into a most mournful expression. "One has to possess an extreme spirituality in order to witness the holy liquification."

"Spirituality, my butt!" Kristen growled.

"The prayer that I always say as I stand before the relic blood on the feast day is—"

Myrella gave a very large yawn for someone so small. "Speaking of feasts, I'm hungry. Let's get out of here before the Snort recovers."

"Yeah, let's go to the Princess Parlor for morning tea," Princess Kinna said. All the princesses rushed out of the Salon de Beauté, leaving Morwenna with her hands clasped in prayer reciting a psalm about blood and vengeance and bad people who "drinketh blood."

Chapter 5

BERWYNNA THE IMPOSSIBLE

Meanwhile, Princess Gundersnap made her way into the Forest of Chimes. She was sweating mightily, for spring had come suddenly and snowshoes were of absolutely no use, not to mention her fur-lined cloak, earmuffs, and mittens. The warm weather would present problems on her return, for the moat would have thawed, and if she did not get back until evening, the bridge would be up and she would have to swim. She had already passed her intermediate swim test last session, an achievement of which she was especially proud.

And now, as she walked in only her petticoats with the

snowshoes and winter gear slung over her shoulder, the temperature was still rising and it was suddenly summer. The Forest of Chimes was yet another one of the odd and slightly magical marvels of the country of Palacyndra that was as unexplainable and perplexing as the fickle seasons that came in no order at all. Lasting sometimes for minutes or days, but rarely longer than weeks, the seasons seemed to be guided by the whimsy of some unknown force.

At first glance, the Forest of Chimes might appear to be any ordinary forest, but if one were to take a closer look, one would observe that the trees did not have leaves but instead clear glass bells. When the wind stirred, the songs of birds mingled in a lovely symphony with the chimes of the bells. It was a place of enchantment. But on this day, the forest was silent, as there was not the slightest breeze to stir the clappers in the crystal bells.

Gundersnap found the tree where Berwynna had appeared to them when she had last visited her with Alicia and Kristen. She sat down on the moss to wait and wait and wait. Noon quickly slid into afternoon, and the light of the summer sky began to leak away, replaced by the pale lavender of twilight. Gundersnap grew more nervous with each passing second. She wasn't worried about being late. That was the other oddity about the Forest of Chimes: time did not behave normally, and although one might think one had been gone for a very long time, one could return and find that only a minute had passed. But what if Berwynna didn't appear? *"G'mutch,"* Gundersnap thought. "I wish the old crone would show up."

"What did I tell you about calling me a crone!"

The princess caught her breath. Before her stood the strange old lady in her garb of leaves and moss and spiderwebs. An owl perched on one shoulder. "An insult always brings me out!" She paused. "But what brings you out? Upon my brother's wand! What a sight you are, scampering about in your smallclothes." She began to cackle madly. "Oh my, if your parents could see you! They'd ask for a tuition refund. And what in the world are those things hanging around your shoulders?"

"Uh . . . snowshoes, ma'am. Alicia lent them to me. You see, it was winter when I left," Gundersnap said in a quavering voice. She took a deep breath and tried to begin. "So . . ."

Berwynna merely grunted in response. "So what? So you mean so so? Or sew sew?"

Gundersnap was becoming more flustered. She'd forgotten how Berwynna often spoke in riddles and tossed words about so that they seemed to take on multiple meanings and become as slippery as a wet frog.

"What have you come for?" the old woman barked.

"Information," Gundersnap blurted out.

"What kind of information?" The old lady screwed up her face and, squinting her eyes, looked fiercely at Gundersnap.

"I have a problem, a big problem." Her eyes began to tear up. *I must not cry! I must not cry.*

"Cry if you want. Tears are free."

Oh darn! thought Gundersnap. She had also forgotten how Berwynna could sometime read one's mind, just step into one's thoughts softly and pick up little fragments and bits and pieces of things.

"I didn't think," Berwynna continued, "that it was a big problem, but a small one, a pony and not a horse."

"You know? What should I do? How can I rescue him before he is killed in battle?"

"Him, just him? Him could be anything. I like to give a problem its proper name."

"Menschmik."

"Ah yes, your mum had no business taking him off like that."

"But what should I do?"

"Do? Dew?" Suddenly sparkling drops of water appeared

to settle on her tangled pile of hair, which resembled more than anything an ill-made bird's nest.

Berwynna stepped closer to the squat princess. Gundersnap felt as if the old lady's oddly colorless eyes were looking straight through her and could see to the bottom of her very soul, could know everything about her, every sadness, every joy, every fear. The owl perching on Berwynna's shoulder shifted its weight and then, as owls can do, spun its head nearly all the way around. Berwynna cocked her own head to look at the owl.

"Uthmore here thinks I should give you a bit of a hint."

"Oh yes, please do!" Gundersnap pleaded. Berwynna raised up on her tiptoes, looked straight into Gundersnap's eyes, and began to speak in a singsongy voice that was as creaky as a door on rusty hinges.

"She thought she saw a horse at first,
The stitches not quite there,
And then she looked again and thought,
A unicorn—beware!
Your mama said that none exist,
These fancies of our dreams.
And yet the stitches left unsewn
Seem to almost gleam.

> *The heart insists, the mind rebels*
> *And says it can't be so.*
> *But listen to your heart I say,*
> *And sew and sew and sew."*

The tiny woman took a step closer to Gundersnap and rose up on her tiptoes again. The colorless eyes seemed to spit the fire of the stars. Then Berwynna sank down from her tiptoes, rocked back a bit on her heels, and gave Princess Gundersnap a smug little grin.

Gundersnap was frustrated.

"But I don't give a fig about unicorns."

"A fig! A fig!" exclaimed Berwynna, and pulled one from her ear. A wasp swooped out as well and began buzzing madly about. "They love figs, don't you know. Lay their eggs in them," Berwynna explained.

"In your ear?" Gundersnap felt a churning in her stomach.

"If I've said it once, I've said it a hundred times: I am a friend of all creatures. If they find my earwax comfy, why not? I'm a decent sort of a landlady. I evict no one."

"But I don't understand what a unicorn has to do with Menschmik."

Berwynna merely shrugged. "How should I know?"

She's impossible! thought Gundersnap.

"Of course I'm impossible," Berwynna replied. "What fun is there in being possible?"

"Were you speaking about my *mudder* in the poem?" Gundersnap asked. "Empress Maria Theresa?"

"Every kid tries to blame her parents. How unoriginal! So don't be getting a bee in your bonnet about mothers." Just then a large bee flew out from a tangle of hair. Gundersnap blinked and suppressed her surprise. *I should be used to this by now,* she thought. Nevertheless, a bee flying out of someone's hair and a wasp from her ear were still alarming.

But the bee and the wasp vanished into the night, and suddenly the edges of Berwynna's body began to grow blurry and smudged. Her face was fading.

"She's dissolving," Gundersnap whispered to herself. *How can she leave me like this?*

"I can, I can." The words echoed somewhere in her head.

"But what am I supposed to sew—a horse or a unicorn?!" Gundersnap moaned in despair. "Oh, come back. Please come back!" she wailed.

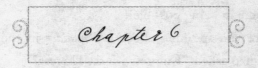

A ROYAL MESS

"Well?" Alicia asked when Gundersnap returned. In fact, less than an hour had passed since she had left, although it had seemed much longer. The princesses were readying themselves for luncheon.

"Where's Gortle?"

"Don't worry. He's not entertaining anyone. He and Lady Merry went out for a sleigh ride. Although now that the snow is gone, they're probably stuck in the mud some-place."

"Did you find her? Did you meet her?" Kristen asked impatiently.

"Yes, I met with Berwynna." Gundersnap sighed as she spoke.

"Oh no!" Alicia exclaimed. "Up to her old tricks, was she?"

"Rather," Gundersnap replied.

"What old tricks—magic?" Myrella asked.

"Not really," Alicia replied. "Berwynna has this annoying habit of speaking in riddles and never actually answering your question, at least not with whole answers."

"So what parts did she give you, Gundersnap?" Kristen persisted.

On her way back from the Forest of Chimes, Gundersnap had thought hard about what she would say. She would have a lot of explaining to do, because she had never revealed to Kristen or Alicia what she had seen that last night of the previous session when they had worked on the unfinished tapestry. She had never told them about the dim lines of the figure of what could possibly be a unicorn. She was not sure why she had not told them. Perhaps it was because she did not believe in unicorns. Or was it because her mother did not believe in unicorns? "Fairy tale nonsense" the empress called them. If her mother said something didn't exist, it didn't! And her mother was usually right.

But then again, her mother had been so wrong about Menschmik. She had said that the pony was a gift. That he belonged to Gundersnap alone and that none of the other fourteen—or was it fifteen—brothers and sisters could ride him. Yet it was her mother who had taken her gift away, taken Menschmik into war.

Could there be some connection between Menschmik and the dim outline she saw in the tapestry? Or could the tapestry, like a cloth version of a crystal ball, foretell what had happened to her pony?

"Are you going to tell us anything?" Kristen blurted out.

Gundersnap turned to them. "I'm going to tell you a lot," she said softly.

"What?" The three princesses pressed around her.

"The tapestry is not finished. Not at all. We must go there as soon as possible. I'll explain on the way."

The cool shadows of the portrait gallery stretched across the stone floor. Hanging in this gallery were paintings of all the princesses who had attended Camp Princess and then been crowned as queens, including Princess Alicia's own mother, Queen of All the Belgravias. Whenever Alicia came into the gallery, she felt as if her mother's eyes were following her.

The four princesses walked directly to the portrait of a princess from long ago who they now knew was, in fact, the very same one who had haunted the South Turret for hundreds of years. On the way Gundersnap explained about the dim outline of a unicorn she thought she had seen in the tapestry.

"So that's the Ghost Princess, the one who helped your bird to sing, Alicia," Myrella whispered.

In the painting this princess wore the typical headgear of the time. A wimplelike coif on her head was wrapped down under her chin, held fast by a coronet, and then over this a full veil fell to her knees. Alicia, Kristen, and Gundersnap were always rather stunned by the old-fashioned garb. And although Myrella had walked through the gallery countless times, she had never really stopped to look at this painting close-up as she was doing now.

"Oh good heavens, talk about last year's fashions—try last century!" Myrella gasped.

"Yes, slightly Middle Ages," Alicia said as she touched the lower edge of the frame of the painting. Myrella looked on in amazement as the portrait mysteriously swung open to reveal a doorway. The princesses passed through and made their way up the spiraling staircase of a turret that no other campers or staff seemed to know existed.

When they reached the top, they were in a dimly lit space. On the wall hung the unfinished tapestry. The princesses' fine needlework from last session stood out against the rest of the tapestry, which was old and faded. It was these stitches in bright colorful thread—made by Alicia, Gundersnap, and Kristen—that brought new life to the tapestry. The picture they had sewn showed a lovely medieval princess standing with a handsome knight in golden armor. At their feet was an empty birdcage. They stood at the edge of the Forest of Chimes and, if one looked very closely, one could see the figure of a very bent little old lady.

"See, Myrella," said Alicia. "That's her—Berwynna, the crone."

"But everything looks finished to me, Gundersnap," Kristen said. "And you're sure that Berwynna said that we should come here and sew something?"

"Say the poem again," Myrella asked. "The sew and sew part."

Gundersnap recited:

> "*The heart insists, the mind rebels*
> *And says it can't be so.*
> *But listen to your heart I say,*
> *And sew and sew and sew.*"

"I don't get it," Kristen said. "What is it that your heart is insisting upon and your mind rebelling against?"

Gundersnap bit her lower lip lightly, and her forehead crinkled into a frown. "It's hard to explain the mind rebelling part. I think it has to do with the unicorn. Empress Mummy taught us that such things were nonsense."

"And what about the heart part?" Alicia asked.

"That's about Menschmik." Her eyes filled.

"But I don't even see the outline of this unicorn that you say is here. Where?" Kristen asked, leaning forward and squinting her eyes at the tapestry.

Gundersnap walked up to the tapestry and touched her finger to the worn cloth. "See right here—now is that a horse or a unicorn?"

The other three princesses came closer and suddenly they saw it. There was something there—definitely.

"I think . . . I think . . ." Alicia began slowly narrowing her eyes as she looked at the outline. "I think it's a unicorn."

"Or perhaps," said Kristen, "it's a half horse, half unicorn?"

"Or a unicorn changing into a horse?" Gundersnap said. She was relieved that at least they saw it.

They stepped back from the tapestry, looked again, and then stepped up close. This went on for several minutes as the four princesses tried to make a shape of the faint figure that at one moment seemed to be one thing and then the next something else.

"It looks like a unicorn to me," said Alicia.

"No, it looks like a horse," said Kristen.

"Maybe," said Myrella.

"There can be no maybes!" Gundersnap replied.

"Oh well, then." Myrella studied the outline again, then turned to Gundersnap. "A horse?"

"Not a horse." Gundersnap sighed. "Not big enough. Just a pony." She felt a twinge deep within her. Then she squared her shoulders. "Enough of this talk. We won't know anything until we start to sew."

"She's right," Alicia said. "Things will become much clearer when we begin stitching."

"But what to stitch?" Myrella asked in a small, exasperated voice.

"Just plunge in," Alicia said. "Remember that's what you told us last session when Gundersnap and I were still afraid of the water and didn't know how to swim. 'Just plunge in,' you kept saying."

Myrella remembered. Both she and Kristen, coming from water kingdoms of isles and marshes, were excellent swimmers.

Just as the last time the princesses had sewn on the unfinished tapestry, there was a row of needles already threaded and tucked into the fabric, as if waiting for the princesses to begin. They each took a needle and then Gundersnap, like a general commanding an army, began to issue orders in a style that would have made her mum proud.

"I'll take the head," Gundersnap said. "Alicia, you take the tail." She pointed to a place on the tapestry.

"I guess that leaves the legs to me," said Kristen.

"No," Gundersnap said. "You're tall, Kristen. Myrella's short. You do the top of the head, the mane, and the ears. And leave the legs and the hooves to Myrella."

"Hooves?" Myrella said with disbelief. She squinted at the tapestry. Gundersnap must be seeing a lot more than any of them, she thought.

They had been stitching for almost an hour when Gundersnap said, "Let's step back and see vot is vot."

The three princesses stepped back and looked at their needlework.

Alicia scowled. "Something's wrong."

"This doesn't look like anything," said Kristen.

"It's not a horse. It's not a unicorn." Gundersnap sighed. "It's a mess."

"A royal mess," Alicia muttered.

"We better go back for now. I must think," Gundersnap said wearily.

The girls made their way down the spiraling staircase out through the secret door, then began walking back through the gallery. They soon heard the clack of feet, and froze in their tracks as they saw the Duchess of Bagglesnort rounding the corner.

"By Saint Jude," Alicia whispered. Saint Jude was the patron saint of desperate situations.

"Hello, Miladies!" the Duchess of Bagglesnort said in an oozy voice. "It's quiet time, is it not?"

"Yes, we were reading in the library," replied Kristen. "About . . . uh, Saint Claudia . . . the patron saint of beautiful women."

"Oh. Bravo. Yes, my dear. Fascinating, is she not?"

"Very," Kristen said, hoping the Snort would not ask any more questions.

"I myself am on the way to the library to research some of my more illustrious family members. You know I am a direct descendant of Simon the Good, who led a crusade to the Holy Land. So I must hurry off."

The princesses breathed a sigh of relief as they watched her wide skirts swish around a corner. "Crusades!" Kristen snarled. "A lousy excuse for war if there ever was one. May a thousand camels relieve themselves on your ancestor's grave, Duchess!"

"Kristen!" Alicia exclaimed.

That evening in the princesses' salon, gloom had settled in. The princesses were troubled and confused about the mess their stitches had made. No one was more troubled than Gundersnap. Had Berwynna misled her? It hadn't been this way last time when they had stitched the Ghost Princess. As soon as they had begun sewing, the picture became very clear. Now it was as if their stitches had been scrambled and made no sense. Had something happened to the tapestry? Why was it misbehaving? Was it no longer magical? All these questions ran through her head, and Princess Gundersnap slept not a wink for the entire night.

Chapter 7

BASIC UNICORN

"You can't cut Basic Unicorn," Kristen pleaded when Gundersnap said she planned to stay behind and work on the tapestry.

"You'll get into trouble," Myrella said.

"I am already in trouble," Gundersnap said. "How can I care about a fantastical beast?" Then she muttered something about not giving a royal hoot about unicorns and that all she cared about was her own tapestry.

"How can you care about a fantastical tapestry?" Alicia rejoined.

A flush crept up Gundersnap's cheeks.

"Touché," whispered Kristen. "Point won."

"Come along now, Gundersnap!" Alicia took the princess's hand and gave her a yank.

"Oh, all right!" Gundersnap said, and then muttered something in Slobo under her breath.

The princesses were to report to the riding counselor and head unicorn wrangler, Lady Frances, known as Frankie. They made their way to the royal stables in the inner ward of the castle, along with a dozen or more other princesses. All were careful to pick up their skirts as they daintily stepped over piles of horse poop.

"Is it true that unicorns drool gold spit when they're nervous?" one princess asked.

"And what about the jewel at the base of their horns?" said another.

"Oh, I think only one in a thousand unicorns has that."

"More like one in a million!"

None of the princesses had ever been on a unicorn roundup. They crowded into the small tack room of the royal stables, where the saddles and the bridles of the ponies were kept. This was where Frankie liked to have her "get ready, get riding" sessions, as she called them. Today, however, it was a little different. When the princesses entered, there were three posters on easels.

Lady Frances came in through another door. She had a loping stride somewhat similar to a horse in a slow canter. Frankie was unlike any other counselor at Camp Princess. She always wore her hair braided into two very long pigtails. On her head she wore a bizarre contraption that had a deep brim and tied under her chin with a leather cord. The weirdest thing of all was that she wore breeches like a man, and then over those, beautiful leather pants. But the pants had no back to them, and instead were tied onto the front of her legs. She called them "chaps," a term few of the princesses had ever heard before coming to the camp.

"All right now, settle down, Princesses. Parisiana!" she bellowed out.

She fired a fierce look at the Princess Parisiana, a pretty girl from the Majestic Realm of Chantillip. "Put a button on it—as in 'louffe'—mouth! Yeah, yeah, I know how to speak Chantillip." Despite Frankie's harsh words, all the princesses secretly admired her.

"Now take a look at these posters," said Frankie. "I want you to understand this." She paused dramatically and pointed to the detailed illustration of a unicorn. "This is a unicorn." She then pointed to the one next to it. "This is not a unicorn. It is an antelope. An antelope is not—I repeat, *not*—a unicorn. Not even a kissing cousin. An antelope has two horns, as you can see from this poster. Not one—duh! Why people confuse them, I'll never know. What other differences do you see?"

Princess Myrella raised her hand.

"Yo!" Royal titles were usually dropped with Frankie. She often addressed them with a "yo" or "y'all," short for Your Highness, Your Majesty—whatever.

"Well, the antelope's horns are curved. The unicorn has a single horn, and it is very straight."

"Right. Now please look at the third poster. Would anyone care to read these facts out loud." A very pretty princess with a mass of frizzy black curly hair that stuck out like an immense halo from her head raised her gleaming dark hand. "All right! Princess Ruby, take it away!"

Princess Ruby began reading the poster aloud.

✳ FACTS ABOUT UNICORNS ✳

- ✳ Unicorns generally travel in herds, but are solitary when they arrive at their destination.
- ✳ Unicorns will not drink from still water.
- ✳ Unicorns are symbols of purity—so don't

think dirty thoughts or speak swears
when around them.

* One touch of a unicorn's horn can stop
  the flow of blood from deep cuts.
* Only young girls can ride unicorns well.
  But men, boys, and old ladies often try
  to with little success.

When the princess had finished, Frankie flipped the poster over. Another princess was asked to read aloud. This time it was Kristen.

✳ FICTIONS ABOUT UNICORNS ✳

* A touch of a unicorn's horn does *not* cure
  acne.
* Unicorns are *not* cupids. They do not
  cause people to fall in love.
* Unicorns do *not* pee, poop, or drool gold.

"And now, princesses"—Frankie placed another poster on the stand—"we have to discuss the unknown." She gave a special and almost mysterious emphasis to the word "unknown." "There are many things said about unicorns that are unprovable. We know not whether they are fact or fiction. I call them 'factions.' Princess Gundersnap, will you kindly read these."

Gundersnap sighed somewhat mournfully and made her way slowly to the poster. Suppressing a yawn, she began to read aloud.

✳ QUESTIONS OF FACTION ✳

- ✳ Can unicorns cover vast distances in very short time, which the ancients called "flash time"?
- ✳ Can unicorns sprout wings and fly?
- ✳ Can unicorns turn blood to rubies?
- ✳ Can ordinary horses or ponies be turned into unicorns?

Gundersnap appeared totally bored and somewhat distracted as she read the faction poster. When she returned to her seat, Frankie stood up.

"Although you might not have known it, given the manner in which Princess Gundersnap read, these factions are considered fascinating, and many scholars have devoted years of research to just these questions and several more factions.

Now, Princess Kinna, can you give us a slightly more lively reading of the other side of this poster."

Frankie flipped the poster, and Princess Kinna from the Queendom of Mattunga came to the front and began reading. Kinna was cocaptain of the Purple team, and if there was ever an enthusiastic, gung-ho princess, it was Kinna. She paused, looked at the poster, and then began reciting it in a rhythmic beat as she slapped her hip and bopped about, making it into almost a song or at least a cheer like the Royal Cheersters would cheer at Color Wars games.

✳ HOW TO TRACK AND CAPTURE A UNICORN ✳

- ✳ Unicorns have a lovely roselike scent. So keep sniffing.
- ✳ Look for the gleam—the gleam of the unicorn's pure ivory horn.
- ✳ When approaching a unicorn, do not look it in the eye. Hum softly and try to think pleasant, sanitary, squeaky clean thoughts.
- ✳ Unicorns are very neat. They avoid mud and slime.
- ✳ Your lariat is made of finest satin. When

throwing it, aim for the horn. If you are successful in your lassoing, drop to your knees instantly and bow your head. The unicorn will then trot directly to you.

* *Never pull on the lariat.* Pulling on the lariat could injure the horn.

"All right, y'all," Frankie continued. "These are some of the basics. We shall be setting off soon. Now, your footmen who usually attend your carriages and horses have already gone ahead to make camp, and I want you all to be ready to leave within the hour. Got that?"

"Yes, ma'am," they all answered in unison.

"Oh, and by the way, I know that in your home kingdoms you are accustomed to riding sidesaddle in your gowns. But not here, y'all. None of this petticoat and gown business. Here we ride western style—facing front. How in the name of Saint Dude do you expect to see anything facing sideways? I've always found that those loose overgowns, kirtles, whatever you call them, are a complete nuisance. And no big wide sleeves, no trains, no veils. We can't have you flouncing around out there on the plains in all that court getup. You'll wear chaps like these over breeches. Your hair shall be braided by the hair maids into two sensible braids. You shall wear a hat—yes, this is a hat, even if you've never seen one quite like it," she said, pointing to the odd thing on her head. "It will stay on when you gallop, and it will protect you from the sun."

Frankie's hat had not quite done the job. She had a solid band of freckles across her nose and stretching from ear to ear.

As they left the stables, Princess Morwenna, who was walking beside Alicia, said, "I don't think it's godly for us to wear these britches and chaps, as she calls them. And to ride western style. Outrageous."

"Whatever!" Alicia muttered.

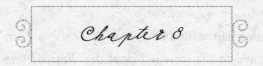

Chapter 8

ROUNDUP

The silk tents in pastel colors glowed under the light of a pale moon. Twenty princesses gathered around the campfire. They leaned against their saddles—the velveteen, super-cushie, butt-friendly princess pony models from the *Royal Outdoor Life Catalogue*. It was a starry night, and as Gundersnap looked at the heavens she thought, *I should be so happy here.* She was out on the plains of Wesselwick tracking unicorns. Drifts of stars flowed through the night. Her difficult mother, the Empress Maria Theresa, was far away. And Frankie was just the best! But she was far from happy. She felt as though she were drowning in a grief as huge as any ocean. *Menschmik! Menschmik, where are you?* She tipped her head back and looked up at the stars. *Please, dear Lord, save my pony.*

Gundersnap settled back now against her pony's saddle and listened to the strange ballad that Frankie was singing. Frankie's sweet, sad song wove into the night and through the stars that seemed close enough to touch.

> *"Oh give me a home where the unicorns roam*
> *And royal gals gallop and play,*
> *Where seldom a flounce is able to bounce*
> *And our hair stays braided all day.*
>
> *Home, home on the plains*
> *Where royal gals gallop and play,*
> *With skirts left behind, our lassos unwind*
> *And our pigtails are flopping away.*
>
> *Oh give me a land where the sky is so grand*
> *And stars from the blackness beam,*
> *Where falcons glide and princesses ride*
> *In search of the unicorn's gleam."*

But where might her dear Menschmik be now, at this very moment? Gundersnap hated to even think about it. He could be in a battle. Yes, they would cover him with leather and all the horse armor, but that would make it even harder for him to gallop. She imagined Menschmik gasping and stumbling across a battlefield, his small lungs crumbling inside his narrow chest. Many of the princesses had set up their lanyard hooks while Frankie sang and were braiding great lengths of satin ribbon using the diamond or spiral braid pattern. But the long satin ribbons lay lank in Gundersnap's lap. She had not braided half an inch.

"Not making yourself a lanyard, lass?" Gortle came up to her. He had come along on the unicorn hunt, helping to set up the tents and doing odd jobs around the campsite.

"I don't have the heart, Gortle. I just can't stop thinking about Menschmik."

"I know, dear, but I think that there's a very good chance, Menschmik being as fast as he is, that the empress won't use him in battle, but only as a messenger pony."

"You're just saying that to make me feel better, I know, Gortle."

Gortle blinked and thought that his mistress knew him too well. "Well, you can always hope, dear. What's life without hope?" He paused, smiled, and then whipped out a lanyard. "Or without rope."

"Where'd you get this, Gortle?"

"I made it for you. Had a feeling you wouldn't be up

to doing one yourself."

"You're too good to me," Gundersnap said, taking the lanyard. She looked at her friend, who now sat next to her sharing the large velvet cushion. The flames of the campfire cast bright shadows across his whiskered face. "Did you always hope, Gortle?"

"Hope for what?"

"Hoped when you were young? Did you hope to grow taller, to not be a dwarf?"

"Of course I did. Don't know a dwarf who hasn't hoped for that." He chuckled softly and looked up at the starry sky.

"But then when you didn't grow, did you stop hoping?"

Gortle's bushy eyebrows shot up. "Stopped hoping for what I couldn't be, but tried to hope for what I could be."

"And what was that?"

"A decent man with some learning. No one in my family had ever read a book. That to me is a lot worse than being short. That's how I got my job in your mum's court. I was the librarian. I could scramble up all those bookshelves good as any monkey, except I read." He laughed.

"So why aren't you still doing that? Why are you just used for tumbling and all that vile silly stuff?"

"Your mum got Arthur."

"Arthur the Giant?"

"Yes, she had wanted him for court entertainment, but he was not very entertaining."

"I can believe that!" Gundersnap said. There was never a man with a more doleful face than Arthur.

"But he was tall and could reach for those books. So I became the entertainment."

"But that's so sad. You loved working in the library."

"Hey, I can still read, can't I? Just have Arthur fetch the books for me now." He paused and then gasped, "Look, a shooting star!"

"I see it!" Gundersnap exclaimed.

"That means good luck."

"I need it." Then she thought, *Or Menschmik needs it!*

"All right, Princesses." Frankie had put aside her guitar and ambled to where the princesses sat at the campfire. "We always set out a watch on roundup to look for the gleam of the unicorns. You can split up into twos and take two-hour shifts until dawn. Anyone spots a gleam, come immediately—that's *boute mooey* in Chantillip, and how do you say 'immediately' in Slobo, Gundersnap?" There was a long pause. Gortle nudged her. "Gundersnap! You paying attention?"

"Oh, sorry, Frankie."

"How do you say 'get me immediately' in Slobo?"

"*Garschmicht*," Gundersnap replied.

"*Garschmicht*," Frankie repeated. "Oh! I like that Slobo talk. It's a language you can really bite into—like a good hunk of meat."

Princess Gundersnap and Princess Alicia agreed to take the shift from two in the morning until dawn.

"Oh, I hope we spot something." Alicia yawned as she and Gundersnap took their posts. "And do you think it's true—this rumor that boys from Camp Burning Shield might be out here somewhere looking for a herd too?"

"Alicia, it's unicorns we're after, not boys. Besides, the boys have no luck with them. Frankie says they can't ride them at all."

"Might be fun to see them try," Alicia said.

"*Ya ya,*" Gundersnap replied in a distracted voice. "Alicia," she said. "You know how my *mudder* does not believe in unicorns."

"As you have said many a time."

"I've been wondering. Do you think that the reason the stitches got all messed up and the tapestry didn't work is because Mudder does not believe in unicorns?"

Alicia looked straight at her friend. "Princess Gundersnap, it is what you believe that counts, not what your mother believes. Do you believe in unicorns?"

"Well, yes, I mean, I think so. Why would we be on

roundup if they don't exist?"

"But do you really believe in them and their magic?"

"Frankie didn't really say anything about their magic. Well, the faction stuff sounds sort of like magic."

"Does she have to say it for you to believe in it?"

Gundersnap furrowed her brow. She turned to Alicia again. "Can magic be practical?"

"Practical?" Alicia sighed. This was so like Gundersnap. "I don't know, but even if it isn't, what does it matter?"

Gundersnap had no answer to that. And what was magic, anyhow? Gundersnap suddenly realized that despite her overwhelming sadness, this night, so different from her life at home in Slobodkonia, did seem almost magical. It was just as she was having this thought that Alicia cried out, "The gleam! I see the gleam!"

Chapter 9

LOST, THEN FOUND!

In less than four minutes, the princesses were into their chaps, out of their silk tents, and mounted on their ponies. In less than five minutes, they were pounding across the plains of Wesselwick. Their pigtails flapped madly as they followed Frankie's lead.

"Yee haw!" Frankie whooped. "The herd is splitting!" She yelled, "Team captains, listen up." She turned around in her saddle and, while still galloping, called back directions. "Crimson team, head due east. Purples, due west."

Nine princesses on the Purple team followed Maggie, the Schottlandian princess known for her superb riding abilities.

"Hey, Gundersnap!" Kristen rose in her saddle. "Get with the program! This way!" She turned to Alicia as they crouched low in their saddles and hammered across the plain. "Good grief—literally grief. She is so distracted by that pony that she went off in the wrong direction!"

"Here, she's coming our way!" Alicia said. "She can't miss those braids of Maggie's." Directly ahead Princess Maggie's braids, the color of paprika, flew out behind her as she rode. Her long body hunkered down low on the pony. She looked like a streak across the breaking dawn as she raced toward the herd.

It was an astounding and beautiful sight to see these magnificent unicorns. Their ivory horns glimmered with a strange light as they sped toward the foothills of the Wesselwick Mountains at the edge of the plains. This was exactly what Frankie had said they would do. If the princesses could get to the unicorns before they entered the forest at the base of the foothills, rounding them up would be much easier.

The unicorns were running in a tight pack. The scent of roses was carried by the dawn breezes, and soon the plains of Wesselwick smelled like a vast rose garden.

For a few moments, it was as if the herd's horns had merged into one luminescent streak of light. But then suddenly the streak melted away.

"By Saint Kippy's last kneecap, they've gone for the woods!" Princess Maggie cursed.

"Who the heck is Saint Kippy?" Kristen asked as they rode along.

"Patron saint of unicorns," Maggie replied, looking back over her shoulder.

"Why last kneecap?" asked Gundersnap.

"Only had one," Alicia answered breathlessly while pressing her pony forward. "One leg, one kneecap, one arm, one hand, one eye, and one horn growing out of his forehead. So naturally he'd be the saint of the unicorns. He is also called the saint of oneness."

"Sounds adorable," Myrella said, crouching her tiny body low in the saddle and keeping her eyes fastened on the herd. So minuscule was the princess that she appeared as not much more than a bump on the back of her pony.

Princess Maggie raised her right hand and gave the signal for them to slow to a trot.

The ten princesses trotted up into a circle at the woods' edge. "Well, we've lost them for now. All we can do is keep sniffing for the rose scent and look for hoofprints. We should meet back here in . . . what do you say, Kinna?" Maggie asked, consulting her cocaptain.

From her waistband Kinna took a watch on a chain. "In thirty minutes," Kinna replied. Then she continued, "The buddy system, remember? Maggie and I will be one team. Rosemary and Hutta, you two go together. Gundersnap and Myrella, Alicia and Kristen. Remember to follow streams when you can."

The buddy teams began to thread their ways through the forest in different directions. Standing up in their stirrups, they poked their noses into the air as high as they could to sniff for roses, but all they smelled was the rich earth of the forest floor.

Gundersnap was lost completely in her own mournful thoughts about Menschmik and, though she had been looking down for hoofprints, her mind was far away as she tried to envision the battlefield in the Empire of Hottompot. Suddenly she noticed a trickle of water. But no, it was more than a trickle, and she wondered how far she had been following it, for very shortly it turned into a lively stream. And then without even lifting her eyes from the ground or her nose into the air, she caught the scent of roses.

"I don't know where she went. One minute she was there. And the next minute, she had just wandered off on her pony." Myrella was almost in tears as she tried to explain how she had lost Princess Gundersnap.

The cocaptains glared at her. "She couldn't have just disappeared," Maggie scolded.

"Didn't you hear her pony walking away?" Kinna asked.

"I don't know! I don't know!" Myrella wailed.

"We came here to round up a unicorn, and now we have to spend time looking for the Princess of Slobodkonia. Zounds! Gundersnap, of all princesses to lose. If her mother the empress finds out, she'll declare war on the camp!" Maggie steamed.

Myrella wailed even harder. "Well, stop your mewling!" Princess Maggie spat the words out.

"Hey! Watch it, Princess," Kristen said sharply as she rode her pony right up to Princess Maggie. Kristen leaned forward in her saddle and looked Maggie straight in the eyes. A kindling energy rustled between the two fiery-haired princesses. Alicia thought she might actually have seen sparks. It certainly looked as if something could ignite any second and the two princesses might burst into flames. "Lighten up, Princess Maggie. Myrella doesn't have eyes in the back of her head. Now let's backtrack to the spot where Myrella first realized Gundersnap was gone."

They had been riding for perhaps a quarter of an hour when they first caught the scent of roses. Quietly they proceeded, and as they came into a clearing, they all gasped at the amazing sight. Princess Gundersnap was standing straight up on top of her saddle near a pond of spring-fed water. She was beginning to twirl her satin lariat over her head. On the other side of the pool was a unicorn, a pure white unicorn, busily drinking. The rose scent was almost overpowering. How Princess Gundersnap stood so steadily in the saddle they would never know. How she cast the lariat from such a position was unimaginable. But silently a loop of pink satin ribbon sailed out across the pool and dropped perfectly over the unicorn's horn. In a split second, Gundersnap was off her pony. She dropped to her knees, humming softly. And, just as Frankie had said, the unicorn began to walk around the pool and head directly toward her.

The other princesses had never beheld such an awesome sight. It was mystical. A glow seemed to radiate from the unicorn when the creature gently placed its head in Gundersnap's lap. The glow began to surround Gundersnap as well as she stroked the unicorn lightly and continued humming. The unicorn lifted its head slightly and nuzzled the princess's chin. Gundersnap's face was bathed in a light of sheer happiness. All the sadness had vanished. Not a trace was left.

Minutes later, with Princess Gundersnap leading the unicorn behind her on the long satin lariat, they set off for the meeting place. As they approached, they saw what appeared to be a large gathering of ponies.

"Hey," Princess Maggie said. "That's Camp Burning Shield's riding team and their jousting team as well."

"Jousting!" exclaimed Kristen.

"Boys!" said Alicia.

"If I told you once, Sir Ralph, I've told you a thousand times." Frankie was shaking a finger at the Burning Shield jousting coach. "In the first place, you shouldn't even be out here on the plains of Wesselwick. Unicorns and boys don't mix. Like oil and water. So now you've caught one and you are such a knucklehead that you decide to have this young Prince Rupert von what's-his-name ride it. Well, he might be captain of the jousting team, but he doesn't know royal diddly-squat about riding unicorns."

"What happened?" Alicia whispered to Parisiana.

"See that prince sitting over there on a log, his arm in a sling? That's Prince Rupert. I guess he tried to ride and was thrown. The unicorn got away, and now he's out for the season—the jousting season, that is. But isn't he cute, even with a broken arm."

"Hot!" exclaimed Alicia and smiled at the prince, then gasped. "Oh, by the grace of Saint Valentine, he winked at me!" she whispered to herself. Alicia could hardly contain her excitement.

Chapter 10

AN INVITATION—AT LAST!

Gundersnap was the only one of the princesses to capture a unicorn, which put the Purples quite far ahead of the Crimsons in the Color Wars. The Crimsons had come close to catching one, but not close enough. With just one unicorn and dozens of princesses, it would not do to have them all learning to ride the creature and care for it. There was simply not enough unicorn to go around, as Frankie put it. So it would be Gundersnap and her turretmates who would learn how to ride the lovely creature and care for it. And if more were captured, eventually there would be a unicorn riding show as part of Color Wars, in which both teams would compete.

As soon as they returned from the Plains of Wesselwick, the princesses of the South Turret began stable duty, the first step in learning about the unicorn and its needs. So although the princesses of the South Turret for the most part did not know the first thing about getting themselves dressed, they would soon be learning how to curry a unicorn, fit a bridle to its head, and strap a velveteen saddle on its back. And although they could no more boil an egg than fly, they were learning how to make clover mash feed for the unicorn.

Lady Merry dozed now in the main salon of the princesses' apartments. She had perhaps fallen asleep from boredom, for all that Princess Alicia had talked about since their return was the handsome Prince Rupert, who had broken his arm.

"Do you think we should send him a get-well card?" Alicia now asked.

"Vot do you mean vee?" replied Gundersnap, barely concealing the impatience in her voice.

"Who are you talking about?" Kristen asked. Her nose was buried in the *Royal Outdoor Life Catalogue*.

"Who else?" Gundersnap sighed.

"Oh, old poopy Ruppie?" Kristen asked. Gundersnap giggled, but Alicia scowled.

"There is nothing poopy about him. He's captain of the

jousting team. I just hope his arm heals in time for our dance with Camp Burning Shield, if that day ever comes," Alicia said huffily.

"I wonder if he jousts with one of these nifty Richard the Lionhearted double-planked shields?" Kristen asked.

"Honestly!" Gundersnap gasped in despair. "And by the way, Alicia, Rupert comes from a very insignificant kingdom. My mother invaded it several years ago, and his father is just a puppet king. Empress Mummy pulls his strings. So get over Rupert."

At just that moment, Gilly sailed into the princesses' salon. She was grinning widely and held a large scroll in her hand. "Good news, Princesses! It's come at last."

"What?" they all cried at once.

"The invitation!" Gilly unfurled the scroll and began to read: "'The Duke of Palacyndra, Camp Master of Burning Shield, does hereby invite the princesses of Camp Princess to our Full Moon Summer Festival and Ball.'"

There was a deafening squeal from Alicia, who shot up into the air, flipping her tiara right off her head. Kristen, Gundersnap, and Myrella looked at one another.

"*Mishtik grashschnik vinghotten,*" muttered Gundersnap, which roughly translated from Slobo meant, "There'll be no living with her now!"

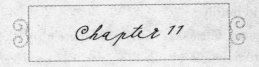

Chapter 11

THE PRINCESSES PREPARE

"Archery contest? There's archery and not just dancing?" Gundersnap asked.

"What about jousting? There's sure to be jousting if there's archery!" Kristen exclaimed.

Lady Merry sighed. "Now, Princess Kristen—archery is one thing, but princesses jousting?" Kristen started to protest. Lady Merry raised a puffy little hand. "Please, dear, we all know that in the Realm of Rolm, things are done differently, and some girls joust."

"Lady Merry, I don't see why not—"

"There will be no jousting for you, my dear. Not another

word." Kristen drooped her shoulders dramatically and moaned. "I am sure there are other sports you excel in."

"Kissing," Alicia blurted out, and all four princesses were seized by convulsions of giggles.

"Gilly!" Lady Merry screamed. "My smelling salts!"

Gortle shook a finger at the girls. "Don't you princesses carry on like that. Giving Lady Merry the fits. Not good. Princess Alicia, you think entirely too much about boys. I know for a fact that you are very skillful with falconry. It says there on that invitation that there will be falconry. And you brought your best falcon."

"Gryffie, yes sir, I did. He's quite good."

"And you, Gundersnap, I know how good you are with the bow. You'll give them a run for their money in the archery tournament. You all need to get out there and practice. Kristen, no one can sail a boat like you. There'll be a regatta. It's not just all fancy dancing and flirting, you know."

"It's not?" Alicia sighed and looked crestfallen.

The days before the journey around the lake to Camp Burning Shield were the busiest of the entire session. Unfortunately, there were extra makeup classes and endless sessions with the hair maids to try out every sort of hairpiece from braids to buns to dangling curls, and some new contrivance called banglets, little corkscrewy things that hung in a fringe over one's forehead and made Kristen looked cross-eyed every time they pinned them in her hair. "I'll take them off and burn them as soon as I'm out of her sight!" Kristen hissed when the Snort turned her attention to another princess. In addition to the makeup sessions, there were endless fittings for ball gowns and tea gowns, in addition to sportswear gowns for various contests and tournaments.

A special shooting outfit was sewn for Gundersnap, a falconry one for Alicia, a new bathing costume for Myrella for the swim meet, and a jaunty sailing gown with gold braid for Kristen. She also insisted on wearing her emerald-studded shark's tooth pendant. This was the highest sailing award given in the junior division of the annual summer Realm of Rolm Regatta. She was also the junior division champion for the winter iceboat regatta, and for this she had been awarded an emerald-studded whale's tooth. But she only wore it for brief ceremonial occasions, as it was quite heavy.

The four princesses of the South Turret stood on small boxes in their salon while four seamstresses and their assistants fitted the various outfits, pinning up hems, taking a tuck here, snipping a sleeve, tacking a collar.

"I really need this to be more off the shoulder," Alicia was saying to the seamstress.

"Off the shoulder—I must gently protest, Your Highness," the seamstress said. She had a beaked nose, and her spectacles perched halfway down the beak made her look like a curious bird. "Whyever would you need this to be off the shoulder?"

"Off the shoulder!" Lady Merry exclaimed. "It's a falconry outfit, Alicia. For mercy sakes."

"That's just the point, Lady Merry. This is my lofting arm."

"What are you speaking of, my dear?"

"Gryffie perches on my right arm. I must hold it up like this." Alicia raised her right arm so that her elbow was level with her nose. "And I must fling him off. I need the garment to be very flexible."

"Hmmm." Lady Merry made a soft vibrating sound that caused her nostrils to flare slightly. Suspicion was engraved on her face.

"It's the truth, Lady Merry. I must have the flexibility."

"Flexibility! I don't like the word. It seems to me that only one arm needs to be flexible, and the shoulder need not be exposed. Seamstress, put an inset in the armpit, some extra material. That's all the flexibility you need."

"Lady Merry," Alicia pleaded.

"Don't 'Lady Merry' me, child. You want to end up like this." She thwacked an issue of *The Royal We* that she had been reading against the arm of her chair.

"What?" all four princesses asked.

"By the lights of Saint Freddy, I have never heard of a naughtier princess than this one," Lady Merry exclaimed.

The princesses had jumped from their boxes, scattering pins and tangles of basting thread, and rushed to Lady Merry's side. Saint Freddy was the patron saint of wayward royalty.

"What naughty princess is it?" Kristen asked.

"Princess Griselda," Lady Merry replied. "She was here a year or so ago. And she has run off with a horse groom!" She slapped the magazine down on her lap. "A horse groom, of all things! And look how she's dressed. You see where bare shoulders in the daytime get you, Princess Alicia?"

In the drawing Princess Griselda was wearing a tightly fitted gown of the latest design.

"What's wrong with it?" Alicia asked.

"The bare shoulders, first of all. That front does not come up high enough. You can see her collarbones."

"It's so this year, Lady Merry. So absolutely now!" Myrella said.

Gortle had just entered the salon and come over to see what they were all looking at. "Very Renaissance, Lady Merry. Get used to it!"

"Fie on this Renaissance. Such nonsense if you ask me— except for a few good plays and paintings. It's just a bunch of hooey. Hooey and hanky-panky with a horse groom! What's the world coming to?"

"Well," Gortle said. "I'm here to fetch Princess Gundersnap. Time to go to the archery field, my dear. The archery master is awaiting you. He says Burning Shield offers some stiff competition, in particular a certain Prince Haraldsvar of Svarlandia."

"May I suggest, Milady, a traditional bow." The archery master, Hawkins, held out a bow toward Gundersnap. "This one should be just the right size and shape for you. You say you've had experience with this one in contests before."

"Yes, sir," she replied, and reached for the bow. Princess Gundersnap wore a rather ancient-looking armguard to protect the inside of her forearm from the slap of the bow-string when it was released.

"But are you sure you would not prefer one of our newer model armguards? That one appears rather . . . er . . ." The archery master searched for the right words. "Rather used."

"Yes, by me. I like it," Gundersnap replied, thus putting an end to the conversation.

The targets had been set up, and at least half a dozen princesses stepped up to the marks. "Now remember, Miladies, the art of shooting requires five steps. To stand properly, to nock, to draw, to aim, and to loose."

It was all archery talk about fitting the arrow's notch to the bowstring, pulling the string, aiming, and then letting go. But before the master had even finished his speech, Princess Gundersnap had let go.

"Bull's-eye!" someone cried. And sure enough, the arrow that the Princess of Slobodkonia had shot was quivering at the very center of the target.

"Bravo! Bravo!" Gortle cried out.

Hawkins himself was impressed. "A champion! I see a champion here. What form!" the archery master exclaimed. Then a nasty echo.

"What form." They all turned around. It was the Duchess of Bagglesnort. Her mouth curled into a smirk. "Yes, Princess. What form!" and she rolled her eyes. A nervous silence fell upon the archery field.

"Ah yes." Master Hawkins spoke nervously. "She has perfect arm placement on the release."

Gundersnap knew exactly what the Snort thought of her

form. She thought Gundersnap was too squat and too chubby, had too many spots on her face, and had hair the color of mud.

"Ah, but it takes more than perfect arm placement," the duchess continued. "What about chubby arms? Well, at least sleeves, yes, bell-shaped sleeves will do the trick," the duchess said, casting a severe eye up and down Gundersnap. "Gundersnap missed an important makeup session in the Salon de Beauté. If anyone needs extra help, it is the Princess of Slobodkonia. She is not . . . er"—the duchess hesitated—"a natural beauty."

"Madame." Gortle stepped up to the duchess. "I would like to suggest—"

"Suggest what, little one?"

Gundersnap's color rose and her eyes began to burn. Gortle raised his hand slightly and gave a sign of caution to Gundernsap. But the duchess did not see this. "There are many kinds of form. This is an archery field. This is where Gundersnap excels."

"Yes, little man, do go on."

A silence suddenly engulfed the archery field. Gortle, with a barely discernible tick of his head and sliding his eyes toward the princess, indicated that perhaps the duchess might want to look to her left as the Princess of Slobodkonia raised her bow and notched an arrow.

Although Gundersnap did not point the bow at the duchess, deadly glints sharp as arrows shot from her eyes. The duchess paled. Gundersnap wheeled about and sent the arrow flying toward the target. "Bull's-eye!" All the princesses whooped.

Chapter 12

THE PRINCESS AND THE PIMPLE

Despite the distractions of the preparations for the Full Moon Ball at Camp Burning Shield, Gundersnap had not stopped worrying about Menschmik. If anything, her worries had increased. How could she be consumed with such trifles as winning an archery contest, or such vanities as which crown jewels to wear with which ball gown, when her pony might lie dying on a distant battlefield? She almost resented the fact that her turretmates were so preoccupied with all the frivolous, pea-brained idiocy that seemed to accompany this venture to a stupid boys' camp.

"*Gemluct fyrstucken grimpoken guzeiten phluglenspritz.*"

She was muttering soft curses to herself about this as she pawed distractedly through a small mountain of pearls that her maid had brought up for her to choose from when a shriek split the air. It came from Alicia's chambers. Gundersnap, Kristen, and Myrella ran from their own chambers into Alicia's. Alicia stood horrified in front of a mirror.

"What is it, dear? What is it?" Lady Merry had managed to heave herself from her rocker and lumber into the chamber. "Goodness, you look as if you've seen a ghost."

"Not a ghost. A zit! I have a zit!"

And indeed she did. A red pimple blossomed on the end of the lovely princess's nose.

"By the grace of Saint Clarice, she has abandoned me," Alicia moaned.

"Saint Clarice?" Kristen asked.

"Patron saint of clear complexions," Gilly answered as she came in with a pot in her hands. Alicia was known for her flawless complexion. She regarded any blemish with a horror usually reserved for leprosy or heart attacks.

"Quick, Gilly, get the snails!"

"The snails!" the other three princesses gasped. They all knew the sickening remedy to clear pimples and had vowed never to succumb to it.

"Right here, Your Highness." She lifted up the pot.

"Had them ready in case of such an emergency."

"Eeew!" Kristen made a sound of disgust.

"This is no time for squeamishness, Kristen. Snails and the salt are required. This is battle. Would a knight go without his armor?" Alicia challenged.

"But squished snails," Kristen said in a weak voice.

It was well known that the very best treatment for pimples was snails squished up and mixed with salt, then applied to the face. It was a remedy far superior to the usual one of rose water mixed with lemon juice.

As nauseating as the remedy was, the four princesses watched with rapt attention when Gilly poured salt into several snail shells, which encouraged the creatures to come out. With a pin she dragged them the rest of the way and then began to expertly mash them up with a bit more salt until they were a fine paste.

"Poor snails." Myrella sighed.

"They don't have a brain," Gundersnap said. "No nerves. Very low engineering in terms of the animal kingdom. A step above algae."

With a small spatula, Gilly began to apply the snail mash to the end of Alicia's nose.

"How long does she have to wear that stuff?" Kristen asked.

"As long as it takes!" Alicia replied firmly. "Please send my regrets to the Great Hall tonight and tell them I shall not be dining, due to a temporary indisposition."

"What's an indisposition?" Myrella asked.

"In this case, a zit," Alicia replied. Holding her head as if it were in a vice, she made her way to her bed, where she carefully lay down. She was as still as one of the reclining statues on a coffin in a royal burial chapel. She closed her eyes. "Do not disturb me."

Gundersnap rolled her eyes and once more thought how stupid all this was. Well, she for one was not going to submit herself a moment longer to the giddy foolishness that permeated the entire castle. She too planned to send her regrets to the Great Hall, but for other reasons: a visit to Berwynna was in order.

Chapter 13

JUST ME?

Luckily there was an almost full moon, and the Forest of Chimes with its glass bells twinkled brightly. It was easy for Gundersnap to find her way to the place where she had last seen Berwynna. She would do as she had previously—stand, wait quietly—then, if Berwynna did not at first appear, think a slightly insulting thought. Insults always brought Berwynna out. It seemed as if several minutes had passed, and so far there was no sign of the little old woman who claimed to be Merlin's sister but apparently was not nearly as good a magician.

"Don't even go there!" The snarl set the chimes to tinkling as Berwynna once again seemed to emerge from the

99

bark of the tree. She was wearing her moss tutu this time, and on her feet she had odd-looking shoes that curled up at the toes into points, with an acorn stuck on the tip of each point. Her hair was its usual mess, caught up in a spider's web, and there were a half a dozen spiders creeping around in it. This time on her shoulder a blue jay perched.

"Go where?" Gundersnap replied.

"You-know-who."

"No, I don't know who." She paused briefly. "Oh, your brother Merlin!"

"Oh yes, *him*." Berwynna's eyes bugged out a bit as she said "him."

Gundersnap understood that Berwynna was very sensitive about her brother and his fame. It had been stupid to compare them.

"Yes, very stupid indeed!" Berwynna said.

Blast! For just a moment, Gundersnap had forgotten that Berwynna could read minds.

"Oh yes, I can! One cannot compare Merlin's and my magic. Merlin is becoming a cultish figure . . . cheap commercialization . . . mass-market magic. I practice a more elegant, upscale, high-end kind of magic." She looked slyly at the princess. "So what do you want?"

"I need to know more. I cannot continue to sew. I had to

stop. Maybe it's a unicorn, but it could be something else."
Once again Berwynna stepped closer and rose onto her tiptoes. The bells, the moon, the stars reflected in her strange
eyes.

> *"Behold the gleaming unicorn*
> *With its ivory spiraling horn.*
> *The bloodied and the lame do kneel,*
> *Yet none but true hearts does it heal.*
> *Is it pony? Is it horse?*
> *What magic happens at its source?*
> *Some are born. Yet some are made,*
> *And some are torn from warfare's blade.*
> *So be you strong of heart and mind,*
> *And the mystery shall unwind.*

And that is all I'll tell you now."

Princess Gundersnap clamped her lips into a firm line.
She dared not ask for more. She knew Berwynna would not
tell her another thing.

"Thank you for what you have told me," Gundersnap
replied. "I'd better go back."

As she made her way back to the castle, she pondered on
the words "be you strong of heart and mind." What did that

mean exactly? Be brave? Be loyal? Be of your own heart and mind? Believe in yourself? But what was her self? Her self had been made by her mother. Was there any little part that was just her own? *Just me?* thought Gundersnap with great wonder now. *Just me!*

When Gundersnap returned to the South Turret, again time had turned funny tricks. Though she had left at dinner and this time felt she had only been gone perhaps an hour at the most, the clock was beginning to chime midnight. Earlier she had made a lumpy arrangement of pillows in her bed that more or less resembled her—a squat princess sleeping on her side with her face toward the wall. By the time the tenth bell struck, Gundersnap had replaced the pillows with herself and, even though she had vowed to stay awake and repeat the odd rhyme Berwynna had spoken, by the sound of the twelfth chime the Princess of Slobodkonia was fast asleep.

Chapter 14

SILK

"You went to see her again?" Alicia asked, examining her nose in the mirror. "What did she say?"

"Alicia, if you don't stop looking at that *ferstucken* zit of yours which is almost gone, I'm not going to tell anyone anything. I'm sick to death of all this fuss over a ball."

"A ball and tournaments," Kristen added. "Yeah, cut it out, Alicia. Menschmik's life is much more important than your dumb zit."

Alicia looked stricken. "You're right. It's just . . . it's just well, I've never had a pimple before and—"

"That is the most pathetic excuse ever!" Kristen exploded.

"Well, the rest of us have. So count it as an educational experience, an experiment in democracy."

"The D word!" Alicia nearly leaped out of her kirtle.

"Democracy?" whispered Gundersnap. In the empress's court, any child was spanked who said the D word.

Kristen just sighed mightily. "Now Gundersnap, what did Berwynna say? Just get on with it. Forget I said anything about the D word."

Gundersnap recited the odd poem of Berwynna's. "It's that bloody part that makes me really scared."

"Say that part again," Myrella asked.

"'The bloodied and the lame do kneel / Yet none but true hearts does it heal.'"

"It's like someone's going to get hurt, isn't it?" Gundersnap stuck her bottom lip out. It trembled a bit. She looked as if she were on the brink of tears. "You think my unicorn is all right?" Gundersnap said suddenly. "Oh no, I don't want to have to worry about him, too!"

Five minutes later the four princesses ran into the stable where the unicorn was kept. He stood in the middle of an immaculate stall that was lined not with hay but moss the princesses had all gathered in the Forest of Chimes. He seemed perfectly fine and whinnied when he saw the princesses.

It was the tradition that whoever caught the unicorn was the one to name the creature. So far Gundersnap hadn't any ideas. Alicia and Kristen had discussed between themselves what name she might pick. They hoped it would not be one of those harsh Slobo words.

"He is so lovely, Gundersnap," Alicia was saying. "May I pet him?"

"Sure," she replied. Upon seeing Gundersnap, the unicorn had trotted right up to her. She dropped to her knees, and the unicorn folded his legs and settled on the moss. Then gently he put his head in her lap while she fed him. It was enchanting to watch the two of them together. Gundersnap, who was usually so plain, suddenly seemed radiant.

"He's is so silky. What will you call him?" Alicia said, stroking his shoulder.

Gundersnap looked up, her eyes absolutely dancing. "That's it. I shall call him Silk."

"Totally ice!" Kristen exclaimed, and clapped her hands together.

"It's the perfect name," said Alicia.

"Gundersnap," Kristen said, "what did it say in that unicorn book you were reading the other day about how you can tell how old they are by their horn or something?"

"Yes, the spirals—you count them."

"Like tree rings?" Myrella asked.

"Not exactly. Because it's not one spiral for each year, but one for every five years."

"And when are they in their prime?" Kristen asked.

"Between forty and sixty years old," Gundersnap replied.

"That seems old," Alicia said. "Horses don't live that long."

"Oh, but unicorns do," Gundersnap replied. "They live well over one hundred years."

"Let's count Silk's spirals," Myrella suggested.

The princesses began counting together: "One—two—three—four—five—six—seven . . ." They paused. "And a half?" Gundersnap looked up, for as they came to the last spiral, it seemed as if it had just begun to emerge from the unicorn's forehead.

"Can we round up?" Kristen asked.

"Well, let's just say he's between thirty-five and forty," Gundersnap replied.

"In other words, almost in his prime," Alicia added.

Just then the trumpets sounded to call them to the Great Hall for dinner. The four princesses each gave Silk a hug and then left the stables. But Gundersnap was troubled. She had hoped to find at least part of the answer to Berwynna's riddle in Silk's stall—but she had learned nothing. She was relieved that Silk was safe and sound, but someone was in terrible danger. She feared it was Menschmik, and that perhaps it was too late for her to do anything. *Maybe we must go back to the tapestry?* But when would there be time? Tomorrow they would be going to Burning Shield.

Chapter 15

THE SNORT MAKES A GRAVE MISTAKE

There was eel pie for dinner that night, a favorite with Gundersnap but not with Alicia.

"I just can't stand the way their little heads poke out of the crust, with those beady eyes. It's like being watched while you eat," Princess Alicia complained to Princess Myrella of the Marsh Kingdoms.

"But," replied Princess Myrella, "someone is always watching you when you eat as it is, Princess Alicia."

"That's true, but it's not usually the thing you are eating. An eel—ick!"

"I myself do not care for eels," the Duchess of

Bagglesnort said in that oozy voice she often used. It gave the four princesses a dreadful feeling. The Snort was going to say something awful, probably to Myrella. It was as if the duchess couldn't help herself—although this was no excuse. "Just mean," Alicia had said once, "mean right down to her supposedly royal bones." There were rumors that the duchess had bought her title—if only they could prove it!

But it was worse than Alicia or any of them could have imagined. For the Duchess of Bagglesnort had suddenly risen from her seat. Actually it seemed as if she had coiled up, and her eyes began to glitter. She looked like a snake ready to strike.

"But I am sure our little Princess Myrella probably loves them dearly—eats them, swims with them and who knows, might even dance with them." She paused, as if she had said something terribly clever. But no one laughed. "Oh, I have a marvelous idea for a little amusement. Why not a charming dance between our little froggy princess and the tiny Slobo dwarf?"

Dead silence. Had not the Snort learned her lesson on the archery field?

No one dared look at Gundersnap. Would she explode? Would she seize the sword that was mounted on the wall near her chair and slice off the duchess's head?

Then, before anyone could say or do anything, the Snort picked Gortle up from where he sat next to Princess Gundersnap and began jiggling him as she walked toward Myrella.

Princess Gundersnap made a spectacular leap right onto the tabletop and roared in a terrifying and deep voice, "PUT HIM DOWN THIS INSTANT IF YOU WANT TO KEEP YOUR HEAD ON YOUR SHOULDERS." She had pulled the sword from the wall.

The Princess of Slobodkonia's hot voice could have blistered the paint right off the Snort's face. "Don't you ever, I repeat, *ever*, touch Gortle again." The Camp Mistress, Queen Mother Adelia Elsinore Louisa, hurried to the table and stood by watching silently. The duchess glanced toward her, a beseeching look in her eyes, as if she hoped the Queen Mum would come to her rescue. She waited for her to scold this rude princess. But the Camp Mistress remained silent.

"I meant no harm," the Snort stammered. She saw something that truly frightened her in Princess Gundersnap's eyes.

"You mean nothing ever." The princess's words fell like cold stones, one by one. "You are nothing. Nothing but a painted shell. A complete twit."

"That will be enough, Princess Gundersnap," the Camp Mistress said. And that was all that was said. Gundersnap was not scolded or punished, much to the Snort's dismay.

Chapter 16

OFF TO BURNING SHIELD

"So you say we are not permitted to wear our hair powdered until we are at least thirteen?" Alicia was asking Princess Parisiana as they rode in the nearly mile-long procession that wound around the lake to Camp Burning Shield on the other side.

"Yes, and here I am just two months short of my thirteenth birthday. It provokes me to no end. In the court of Chantillip, we permit eight-year-old girls to powder their hair."

"Eight-year-olds!" Princesses Gundersnap and Kristen both exclaimed at once. The four princesses of the South

Turret were riding with Princess Parisiana. Princess Morwenna and the other nasty princesses of the North Turret rode directly behind them.

"I don't approve of any of it," said Morwenna. These were the first words she had spoken on the ride. It was a perfectly beautiful day. It had been winter at dawn but winter had vanished to be followed by what was called "sudden summer." Sudden summer simply meant that spring had been skipped entirely—no daffodils, no spring chickadees—but now the trees were a deep deep green, the sun hot, and the lake water warm—warm enough for swimming.

"Princess Morwenna, what *do* you approve of?" Alicia turned in her saddle and asked.

"I approve of long hours of prayer. I approve of fasting one day a week. I approve of crusades. And most of all, I approve of my patron saint, whose medallion I wear around my neck. This is the only ornamentation I need," she said, touching the bronze disk at her throat.

Princess Gundersnap guided her horse closer to Morwenna to see the medallion. "It's only a baby on that medallion. A baby saint?"

"Oh, not Saint Rumwald, puleeze!" groaned Kristen.

"Saint Rumwald?" Alicia asked.

"You know the one, Alicia." Kristen grimaced. "Poor kid lived just three days. On the third day he announced, 'I am a Christian' and promptly died."

"You're wearing the image of a dead baby around your neck?" Alicia was shocked. "Totally gross!"

"I agree," said Princess Parisiana.

"And I disagree." Princess Morwenna's face had not changed expression. "It is not gross. It is divine. To know what you are when you are just three days old is a gift of God."

"*Bahksmutch!*" Gundersnap exclaimed.

"Baaawhat?" Kristen asked.

"*Bahksmutch*. It means 'baloney' in Slobo. And saying a dead baby is divine is simply baloney—*bahksmutch*." Gundersnap spat out the word.

This perhaps was the most philosophical discussion that had ever occurred among the campers. Morwenna's face hardened into a tight little mask. Her eyes got all squinty, and her mouth became a thin grim line. "I take grave offense at this. I shall report you to Camp Mistress, Queen Mother Adelia Elsinore Louisa." Then, as she rode off to find the camp mistress, she paused and turned around in her saddle. "*Abi in malam rem!*" which in Latin meant, "Go to the devil."

But Gundersnap, not to be undone, trotted right up to her and said, *"Abi conbiba ovo,"* which meant in Latin, "Go suck an egg."

Princess Morwenna galloped off in a fury.

In the distance they saw silk tents and pavilions against the flawless blue sky. The colors were magnificent—pink, purple, fiery orange, bright yellow, sapphire blue. And from the top of each tent, snapping in the breeze, were the banners emblazoned with royal crests of the princesses.

"I hope we all get to be together in the same tent," Myrella said.

"Let's hope that Morwenna is not with us." Kristen sighed.

Just at that moment, Lady Merry von Schleppenspiel's reinforced carriage drove up. She ordered her driver to stop and motioned the princesses over. She was trying very hard to arrange her naturally cheerful face into a stern visage. "Miladies, I have been hearing reports of nasty exchanges in Latin. Princess Morwenna is quite upset. She is requesting to go to the nearest convent to pray for your souls."

"That's totally lame," Kristen said under her breath.

"She's no more praying for us than we are for her," Alicia

whispered back. "She just wants to get out of going to the ball."

"Now there is to be no more of this. Nothing is so unattractive as a waspish tongue—even in Latin." Lady Merry shook a plump finger at them, then ordered her driver on.

"At least if Morwenna stays at the convent, there is no danger of her in our tent," Kristen muttered. They were approaching the tents now.

"Look!" cried Alicia. "Look! Princes!"

And indeed, what seemed like a legion of princes was riding toward them, each prince bearing a garland of roses to present to the princesses.

Chapter 17

A ROYAL DILEMMA

Princess Gundersnap watched as Alicia danced a very popular circle dance known as the pavane. It looked easy enough. Each princess, holding the hand of her princely partner, made a circle around him. Gundersnap nearly laughed as she saw how the tiny Princess Myrella had to stand on tiptoes while she held the hand of her prince. And even on tiptoes, her hand barely cleared the kneeling prince's. But she seemed unconcerned about her short stature. Short, however, was different from squat and thick. Gundersnap had many fewer pimples on her face than she had last session, and she hadn't even used the squished snail remedy. The one good thing she had learned in makeup had helped. It was a paste made of talc, white chalk, and egg whites, and it covered the worst of the pimples. But it made her face feel very much like a thin porcelain teacup. She was afraid it might crack at any moment.

The dance had finished and another began. This was a lively one, and it required quite a bit of jumping about. Princess Kristen had seized a prince by the hand and dragged him out onto the dance floor. *She is so daring!* Gundersnap wished she had the nerve to just go up and ask a prince to dance. Kristen towered over her partner, but soon they were both leaping in the air. The princess's fiery red hair, which had been braided over each ear and looked like twin pastries, began to come loose. Her shark tooth tiara was slipping down onto her forehead at an angle some might call jaunty for a hat. It was completely idiotic for a tiara.

"By the bones of Saint Vitus, I have never seen such a princess! What am I to do with her?" Lady Merry von Schleppenspiel had her attendant put down her sedan chair by Gundersnap.

"What's wrong?"

"Princess Gundersnap, you call that dancing? Look at her! It's as if Princess Kristen is going to ignite—explode—a royal conflagration! No, a hectic complexion does not serve well."

She's having fun, Gundersnap thought. *And how,* she wondered, *can I have fun when Menschmik might be dead or dying?* Just as she was thinking this dismal thought, she felt a tap on her shoulder, and a voice from behind her said, "May I have the next dance, Princess Gundersnap?" Gundersnap turned and blinked. A prince stood by the chair where she was seated. He was not squat or thick, nor did he have spots. She blinked once more and he asked once more, "May I have the next dance, Princess Gundersnap?" The princess felt a poke in her side. It was Lady Merry poking her to answer. But her voice seemed to have disappeared. Lady Merry poked her a second time. Finally Gundersnap replied, "Why?" At that moment Lady Merry swooned in her chair.

"Because I thought you might like to dance," said the prince.

"Yes, I would," Gundersnap said in a dazed voice.

She then moved to the floor to dance a galliard with Prince Haraldsvar of Svarlandia, a country her mother had not yet even invaded.

"He loves archery!"

"He's the one who is going to be in the tournament?"

Gundersnap nodded solemnly to Alicia and Kristen.

They had returned from the ball and were sitting in their beds in the lavender silk tent they had been assigned to.

"So what's the problem?" Kristen asked. "You both like the same sport."

"But it is a problem. I see it," Alicia said thoughtfully, and scratched her head.

"I don't see at all," replied Kristen.

"They're in competition," Alicia said.

"Exactly!" Princess Gundersnap exclaimed. "Vot am I to do? Do I try and beat him or lose to him?"

Kristen's mouth dropped open in disbelief. "Come again! Did I hear you right? Beat him or lose to him? Is that a question? You beat him! Is the sun yellow? Is the grass green? The sky blue? Duh! You beat him."

"But it's more complicated than that," Gundersnap said.

"How?"

"Empress Mummy? This is truly a dilemma."

"What kind of dilemma?" Myrella asked.

"A royal one," Gundersnap said. "You see, I think I remember Empress Mummy talking about making a match between Glocknia, my third-oldest sister, and this prince's older brother. If that happened, it would save her the trouble of an invasion. And if I beat him, it could ruin the prospects—Glocknia's prospects, that is."

Kristen's face crinkled into a grimace of pure disgust. "You cannot be expected to plan your sports around the possible marriages of your sisters and brothers."

Just then a tent maid sent by Lady Merry to remind the girls of their prayers entered. The three princesses scrambled from their beds and knelt. On this night each princess prayed to a different saint.

Princess Alicia prayed to Raphael, who was not just a saint but also an archangel, the angel of romance and love. Princess Alicia had danced with at least twenty princes that night and she felt all fluttery inside. She just loved love.

Princess Kristen prayed to Saint Sebastian, the patron saint of archers, to for heaven's sake knock some sense into Gundersnap.

And Princess Gundersnap prayed to her mother's patron, Saint Elizabeth, the patron saint of the battlefield. "Please, revered lady, what would Empress Mummy have me do? I don't want to spoil everything, but then again, I really love archery, and I really like Prince Haraldsvar. Do you think he would hate me if I beat him? Would Empress Mummy simply blow up if this wrecked Glocknia's chances? What am I to do for the empire? What am I to do for myself? Just me? Will the prince like me more if I lose to him than beat him? And Menschmik—please, dear Lord, protect my dear pony."

Chapter 18

THE TOURNAMENT

"Don't switch bows, Gundersnap. You're used to shooting with the Dreamcatcher Five Hundred." Kristen had just burst into the archery tent where Gundersnap was being dressed for the tournament. Over a green and white striped flowing skirt, she wore a snappy darker green fitted jacket, and in her sports tiara there was a vivid red feather. Kristen proceeded to give her a pep talk.

"Now I know you're upset about Menschmik, but Gundersnap, you're just going to have to put him out of your mind for a little bit. You need to concentrate on this tournament. You know, if you win it counts toward our points in Color Wars."

"It does?"

"Yes. So you're doing this for the Purples and not just yourself." Gundersnap nodded solemnly. "And promise me there will be no more talk about not winning because of all that nonsense about your sister getting married and your mother's invasion plans and all that."

Gundersnap nodded, but she knew it would be hard. Kristen took a step closer and looked her right in the eye. "Gundersnap, go out there and shoot!"

Princess Gundersnap walked onto the archery field. She wore a quiver of arrows on her back. She carried her Dreamcatcher 500, and as she stepped up to the mark, she flexed it a few times. On one side of her was a prince whose name she did not know. On another side was Princess Parisiana, a fair shot, but not nearly as good as herself. Prince Haraldsvar was on the far side of Parisiana. A bugle was blown to announce that the first flight of arrows could begin.

Princess Gundersnap closed her right eye. With her left eye, she looked through the little gap in the bow, the bow sight, focusing on the center ring of the target. *"Grusschum, grusschum."* She repeated the word in her head. It meant "steady, steady" in Slobo. She raised her elbow and began to draw, then let loose the arrow. Not a bull's-eye but close.

Each contestant would shoot three full quivers of arrows. She was uneven on the first quiver, but by the second was improving steadily. And by the third quiver, she had advanced to second over all in the contest, just two arrows behind Prince Haraldsvar. She could feel Kristen's eyes boring into her. But she could also hear an ominous rumbling voice in the back of her mind—the voice of her mother, Empress Maria Theresa of All the Slobodks. Doubt suddenly washed through her like a tidal wave. Should she try and win? All night she had fretted.

"Princess Gundersnap, an urgent message from your mother the empress." A messenger had rushed up just as she nocked an arrow.

What in the world! Has the Hottompot invasion failed? She put down her bow and walked to where the messenger stood with a sealed letter. He bowed and handed the letter to her. Gundersnap opened the letter and saw her mother's familiar script.

Lose the match!

Love and kisses,
Mummy, Empress Maria Theresa of All the
Slobodks

Gundersnap blinked in disbelief. *She must have spies here all over*, Gundersnap thought. *She's worried that if I beat him, it will spoil her plans—her marriage plans for Glocknia and the prince's older brother.* It was as if her mother the Empress not only invaded countries but her own children. *She's a royal control freak!*

And deep within Gundersnap, a small royal rebellion began to smoulder. Then rage erupted. *"Bahksmutch!"* Gundersnap spat the word out. She picked up her bow and marched to the shooting line. Never had her concentration been finer. It was as if her entire body had merged with the bow. There was no separation between the bow and herself. She nocked the arrow, squinted one eye shut, aimed, and released.

"Bull's-eye!" the crowd roared.

She drew another arrow from her quiver. Her rage at her mother was not a distraction at all, but burned within her, igniting every muscle. She was the bow, and the bow was her. Her vision had never been sharper, her hands steadier. Her fingers pulled taut on the bowstring. Its tension resonated with the fire burning inside her. She released the string and the arrow flew true.

"Bull's-eye!" the crowd roared again.

Gundersnap pulled a third arrow from her quiver and

nocked it. She knew even before the arrow struck. The world went silent, but she felt a glow like gold shimmer within her.

"Bull's-eye!" the spectators screamed.

Kristen ran to her and picked the squat princess up in her arms. "You won! You won!"

But she had done more than simply win. She had shot a golden flight, three bull's-eyes in a row.

Prince Haraldsvar made his way over. He bowed and smiled. "May I have the honor of the first dance tonight at the masquerade ball?"

"You still want to dance with me?" Gundersnap asked.

"Oh mercy!" muttered Lady Merry. "Did I hear that right?"

"Of course. How often does one have a chance to dance with a princess who has shot a golden flight?"

Gundersnap felt a storm of butterflies rising in her tummy. "Oh," she said, and smiled a most dazzling smile.

They were just beginning the fireworks display and Princesses Gundersnap, Alicia, Kristen, and Myrella were about to take off their masks, for their costumes were quite hot. Alicia had gone as a Gypsy. Gundersnap went as a Celtic sprite named Orla, which meant "gold queen." She carried a quiver with three golden arrows and wore golden wings. She knew her mother would not approve of Orla. The empress thought sprites and fairies and winged creatures with human bodies in general were stupid and a waste of time. Kristen went as a pirate queen who was said to have lived many years ago and plundered ships in all the seven seas. In a scabbard that hung at her side, she carried a sword.

"Look," said Princess Parisiana, who was sitting near them. "That must be Myrella dressed up as an ugly old wood sprite."

"No, it can't be. Myrella went as a moon maid. She's all in silver and diamonds. Where are you looking?" Gundersnap asked.

"See over there." Parisiana pointed to a tiny figure who was making her way across the lawn. "No one else is that tiny."

Oh yes she is! all three princesses thought at once. It was Berwynna! And at just that moment, Myrella appeared. Kristen grabbed the tiny gleaming princess, and with Alicia and Gundersnap they sped to the edge of the lawn, leaving Princess Parisiana wondering what in the world it was that had made them take off like that.

Berwynna, however, seemed to have dissolved into thin air. "She mustn't have wanted to meet with us out in the open," Alicia said.

"But where could she have gone!" Myrella stomped her

foot. "Shoot, I haven't ever seen her and all of you have!" Her anger made her diamonds shimmer even more.

"She's got to be around here someplace," Gundersnap said. "Look at that big tree over there!" Alicia pointed at an immense oak with low branches that flowed over the ground like dark rivers in the night.

The four princesses ran over. There on one of the branches, with her short legs dangling in the night, was Berwynna.

"I thought you'd never come!" she exclaimed.

"What are you doing here?" Gundersnap asked.

"Exactly what am I doing here? Out of the Forest of Chimes, exposing myself on a lawn with dancing princesses and princes? Only an emergency would bring me out like this. Why can't you be where you belong?"

"Where's that?" Kristen asked. Gundersnap was beginning to have a horrible sinking feeling deep in her stomach.

"In the hidden turret at the tapestry!" She paused. "And Gundersnap, a word for you."

"What?" Gundersnap's voice was a raw whisper of sheer terror.

Berwynna began in her creaky voice.

> *"Take that pouch with threads of gold*
> *To make your stitches thick and bold.*

Then a picture will appear:
A creature hurt, a creature dear.
On wings like silk you then will fly,
And let us hope that he'll not die."

"Menschmik!" The name ripped from Gundernsap's throat in an agonizing sound.

"Holy monk bones, we're in the wrong place! We should be back at the castle, not here at this stupid boys' camp!" The princesses looked at Alicia in amazement. This indeed was a turnaround for the Princess of All the Belgravias.

Before the moon had risen, the girls were on their ponies riding hard back to Camp Princess.

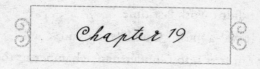

DROPS OF BLOOD

As they slid off their ponies, Kristen, Alicia, and Myrella were peppering Gundersnap with questions.

"Did you understand the verse?"

"What's the wings like silk?"

"I don't get the pouch of gold. Whatever is the pouch of gold?" Alicia asked.

"I told you. Remember when Gortle brought me the letter about Menschmik, he also brought me the clippings from Menschmik's mane? Menschmik's mane looked like pure gold. That's why I called him Menschmik. It means 'bright as gold' in Slobo."

"You have to thread the needle with the hair from his mane, then?" Myrella gasped in excitement. "That's probably why it didn't work last time."

"Yes! It was a mess," Gundersnap said.

They ran first into Gundersnap's chamber in the South Turret. From one of her bedposts hung the very ordinary-looking leather pouch with strands of Menschmik's mane. She grabbed it and they dashed out, down the stairs, through the long corridor, and into the portrait gallery.

"Hurry up! Hurry up!" Gundersnap ordered, almost dancing on her toes in front of the portrait of the Ghost Princess. It seemed to be opening more slowly than ever. At last the portrait swung wide open to reveal the winding staircase to the hidden turret. But it seemed again as if everything were moving painfully slow, as if in a bad dream. Gundersnap muttered under her breath that the number of stairs seemed to have doubled since they were last there.

Her hands were shaking so hard when they arrived that she could not thread the needle. "Here, let me do it," Myrella said. With her tiny hands and fingers, she quickly had four needles threaded with the golden strands from Menschmik's mane.

They all began sewing furiously. The picture seemed to grow and grow around the stitches they had originally sewn. Alicia, who was working on the head of the creature, blurted out, "It's definitely not a pony. It's a unicorn."

Then Kristen began to squint hard and sew faster. "This is unbelievable. This is totally ice. What we thought before was a complete royal mess isn't at all."

"What is it?" Myrella stood on her tiptoes.

"It's Gundersnap! She's riding the unicorn!"

Then there was a small, sharp yelp. The three princesses turned toward Gundersnap. There were spots of blood on the tapestry.

"Did you prick yourself? Here, let me see," Alicia asked.

"No! I did not prick myself. I sewed those. The gold thread turned red. I am stitching blood drops. They are drops of blood. Menschmik's blood!"

"The rhyme, the rhyme," Kristen whispered. "Say it again. What does the rest mean?"

Gundersnap began reciting the verse once again, slowly this time, as if she were almost chewing on every word.

> "Take that pouch with threads of gold
> To make your stitches thick and bold.
> Then a picture will appear:
> A creature hurt, a creature dear.

On wings like silk you then will fly,
And let us hope that he'll not die."

"SILK!" all four princesses exclaimed at once.

"Of course!" Gundersnap's eyes widened and sparkled with new hope. "Remember that was the one of the things Frankie said no one was sure about—how unicorns could sometimes travel vast distances in something the ancients called flash time."

"Well now's the time to prove it," Alicia said.

"Yes." Kristen nodded. "Fact or fiction?"

In the stables the three princesses helped Gundersnap prepare Silk. The unicorn stood patiently as Kristen tightened the girth of the velvet saddle and Gundersnap fitted the bridle into his mouth. The scent of roses was strong in the stall. It seemed that Princess Myrella was the only one who had truly kept her wits about her as they completed sewing the scene of the tapestry. She ticked off the important points. "The battlefield is on a peninsula that juts out into the Hottom Sea. There is a forest on the west side, the side that you'll be approaching from, and there is moss, which is where the drops of blood were. So if you follow those drops of blood once you get there. . ." She hesitated. "Well, that's where he'll . . . Menschmik will be."

"I wish we could go with you," Alicia said.

"If we had only captured more unicorns." Kristen sighed. "Imagine it—the four of us riding together."

"But do you know the way to Hottompot?" Alicia asked.

"Certainly. Mummy always gives us very complete geography lessons on any kingdom she is planning to invade. It is part of our strategic war unit, taught by herself and her best general, Commander Gokinblat. I know the place like the back of my hand."

"But will Silk know how to get there?" Myrella asked.

"If I guide him right. If I ride him well. We will get there," Gundersnap replied confidently.

"But how will you ever get Menschmik back?" Kristen asked.

"I'll figure that out when the time comes. First I must save him. Then I must bring him back, and he will never, ever be in battle again."

Then Alicia, who was holding the reins of Silk's bridle as Gundernsap mounted, looked up at the squat little princess who seemed to glow the second she settled on the unicorn's back and said softly, "Gundersnap, I think you are beginning to believe in magic—practical or not."

"The heart insists!" Gundersnap smiled broadly.

Chapter 20

WHEN FACT MEETS FICTION

Kristen opened the gates of the corral and Gundersnap raced through. The three princesses watched but only briefly, for within a few seconds Gundersnap and Silk had disappeared over the horizon. The gleam persisted for several seconds, as if a sun had just set, even though it was midnight. The princesses, still waving, could just barely smell the lingering scent of roses that stirred in the wake of the unicorn, and then the gleam was gone.

"Well, I guess that's one faction proved." Kristen clapped her hands together as if to punctuate what she was about to say. "Unicorns can cover vast distances very quickly. Maybe she should have named him Streak instead of Silk."

The princesses planned to return to Camp Burning Shield before they were missed and, of course, they had to hatch a plan to cover Gundersnap's absence.

"Why don't we just say," Myrella spoke up, "that the note she received on the archery field suggested that there was some emergency, and her mother required her presence in court. It's sort of true, after all."

"You're right," Alicia said. "And we can tell Gortle the truth. He'll understand, if anyone will."

"It's a fact all right!" Gundersnap whispered to herself as she saw great hunks of a large continent disappear under her. She hunkered down flat against Silk's mane. Sometimes she was not sure if Silk's hooves were even touching the ground. But was it really flying? And so far there were no wings. They were traveling east, and soon she saw water ahead that must, she guessed, be the sea of Hottompot. Reaching out into that sea like a long, crooked finger was the peninsula where the battlefield lay! Gundersnap felt her heart beat wildly. They had made good time, but there was still a long way to go, for they must follow the contour of the shoreline all the way around to the peninsula. She heard Silk breathing hard. "Oh, dear Lord, don't let his breath give out now."

But there was an ominous deep rumbling in the unicorn's chest, and she felt the pounding heart skip a beat and then another. "Oh no . . . Oh no," Gundersnap moaned as his gallop slowed.

Then she felt a strange movement under her calves. She looked down. *"Vyne Vott! Berfluggen splurplunkne faction. Ingrotz Silkmi hoff!"* Which roughly translated from Slobo means, "My Lord! A faction comes true and is not a fiction. Silk is growing wings!" She moved back in her saddle to give the wings full range, and soon she felt herself and Silk leaving the ground. Then, caught on a warm updraft, they began to float higher and higher and were soon over the sea of Hottompot. The wind rushed by her ears in a satin rustle. A wave of moonlight swept across them as Silk flew, and overhead stars scattered and broke the night into one immense sparkling flower. Silk's wings had unfurled completely now and were glorious to behold. Transparent, with flushes of iridescent colors near the edges, they glimmered in the night.

But beneath her she saw a battle raging, and soon they began their descent. Settling in a thickly wooded area on the fringes of the battlefield, they could hear the din of war. Great bonfires burned where gunpowder kegs had exploded or the clashing armies had attempted to burn each other's supplies and weapons. The forest itself was out of reach of the flames, but it was nonetheless bright with the fiery glow of the battlefield. The sound of cannons and muskets being fired was deafening.

Where to begin? Gundersnap thought. *I must look for the drops of blood.* She closed her eyes and tried to remember the tapestry in the hidden turret. She could picture those drops of blood so clearly. They glistened now in her mind's eye, bright as rubies, rubies on moss. "We must look for the moss first," she whispered to Silk. She dismounted and began to walk, leading Silk with satin reins.

It was not long until she found a patch of moss and soon another patch and another and another, until there was a soft moss path. Then, on a sprig of a small white flower called moondrops that poked through the moss, she saw the first spot of blood. She bent down and touched it. "It's still warm!" she whispered to Silk. Her face was pale with fear. "We'll follow this trail. I see more drops of blood ahead."

With her heart beating like thunder, Gundersnap pushed on. She had not gone far when she heard a weak whinny between the blasts of cannon fire, followed by a groan. Her eyes opened wide in horror. "Menschmik!" she cried. She pushed aside a low hanging branch and saw her bloodied and panting pony sprawled on the ground.

Gundersnap dropped Silk's reins and fell to her knees beside the pony. His eyes were glassy with fear but seemed to soften as his mistress stroked his head. There was a terrible gash on his head that was bleeding freely.

Just then a large, familiar shadow slid across the fire-stained night.

"Myshussenfreit! Grott mykin! Shussenfreit schussenfreit nincompoopen." Gundersnap heard the words and could hardly believe it.

Gutten grieffen gobben ich stynken Mummy! The shadow was that of her mother in her full battle dress—metal breastplate, her chain-mail gown, and the helmet with the horns of the giant Slobodkonian bull. She was riding her great warhorse, the charger Thrompen Monschtark, or Thunder Monster. They were apparently looking for wounded and dead, and any enemy weapons they could find scattered about. Gundernsap began to tremble uncontrollably as she heard the crunch of footsteps nearing. *Scouts! She's sending in scouts to search.* She knew that the rule of the battlefield was that badly wounded animals—warhorses or ponies—were killed instantly. Menschmik was badly wounded.

The footsteps were coming nearer and nearer. Suddenly Gundersnap felt Silk's head nuzzling her shoulder. "Calm yourself, calm yourself," he seemed to be saying. Just before the scout stepped out into the clearing, Gundersnap slid behind Silk. She heard a small gasp. She peeked around. The scout was Frizzmor, a favorite of her mother's. *"Eininhorken!"* he blurted out. He turned around and rushed to where the empress waited on her charger.

"Empress minghotten styrnofkein ingen eininhorken!"

He was telling the empress that he had seen a unicorn, but said nothing of Menschmik. Was it possible that he had not even noticed the poor animal? Suddenly Gundersnap heard the unmistakable, loud, raucous, hysterical laughter of her mother.

"Eininhorken schneer vissen bish vyn vott idiot nincom-poopen." The other soldiers accompanying her began to laugh as well, for when the empress laughed, everyone laughed.

This is unbelievable, Gundersnap thought. Her mother did not believe in unicorns. Therefore they did not exist. Therefore anyone who did believe in them was not simply impractical but a fool, an idiot, and a nincompoop, and she would never even deign to go look. The commander of one of the fiercest armies on earth, commander in chief of *Operazynggen Bluffyn Klompen*—which translated from Slobo meant "Operation Blow 'Em Up and Stomp 'Em

Out"—would not go into a woods to chase fairy tale creatures. No siree, not Maria Theresa, Empress of All the Slobodks.

The shadow receded. Gundersnap stepped out from behind Silk, whose head was bent low over the wounded pony. And now it was the princess's turn to gasp. The terrible gash in Menschmik's head had stopped bleeding. She was stunned as Menschmik began to raise himself to his knees. She blinked and inhaled sharply. Where the pony had lain, there was a scattering of rubies. But Gundersnap would have traded all the rubies in the world for what happened next.

Silk bent his head again, and his horn touched where the gash had been on the pony's forehead. Something different was happening. The skin was healing, but a bump was pushing up beneath it. Gundersnap's eyes widened as she realized that she was witnessing a kind of miracle. There was magic in the woods, and slowly a horn began to emerge from Menschmik's brow.

It was a short little horn with only two rings, one for each of the five years Menschmik had lived.

Gundersnap turned to Silk. Her eyes welled with tears. "He shall live many more years, for now he is a unicorn. Empress Mummy will never be able to take him away again."

And it was true. On this night, near a blood-drenched and fiery battlefield, a unicorn had been made. And Gundersnap's mother, the empress, did not believe in unicorns. Thus Menschmik would be safe forever after.

Gundersnap climbed on Menschmik's back. His wings were just unfolding. Together the princess and the new unicorn rose into the night with Silk at their side, the words of Berwynna like a song filling Gundersnap's head.

> *Behold the gleaming unicorn*
> *With its ivory spiraling horn.*
> *The bloodied and the lame do kneel,*
> *Yet none but true hearts does it heal.*
> *Is it pony? Is it horse?*
> *What magic happens at its source?*
> *Some are born. Yet some are made,*
> *And some are torn from warfare's blade.*

Chapter 21

A GLOW IN THE DAWN

Princess Kristen was leaning out the window of her chamber. She could not sleep. They had been back an entire day and a night from Camp Burning Shield and, although the excuse they had given for Gundersnap's absence was generally accepted, she was beginning to worry. Gortle had to make himself scarce, as he was supposed to have been the one to escort the princess back to the palace in Slobodkonia.

Dawn was just breaking when suddenly, on the hill where the princesses had last seen Gundersnap, Kristen saw a glow. It was as if the hill were powdered with the gold of the rising sun. But it was not the sun. Kristen ran for her high-powered binoculars that had just come from *Royal Outdoor Life Catalogue*. She pressed them to her eyes. *It's her! It's her, and there are two unicorns!* Immediately she rushed into Alicia's chamber and then to Myrella's closet.

"She's coming back. We've spotted her!" Myrella sat up so suddenly in her draw that she smacked her head. "Ouch! Gundersnap's back?" she asked.

"Yes, and it's summer. We'll just swim the moat. No one will be up for hours."

"Let's get Gortle!"

They ran to another closet and knocked on a drawer in it. "Get up, Gortle, get up! She's back!"

"Oh, bless Saint Gubbins!" he exclaimed. Saint Gubbins was the patron saint of dwarves.

The three princesses and the dwarf raced down the banks of the moat, swam across it, and struck out across the field. Gundersnap spotted them immediately and raced forward. She slipped off Menschmik's back and hugged the wet princesses and the wet dwarf. "This," she exclaimed, "is Menschmik, believe it or not!"

"I'd recognize him anywhere!" Gortle said joyously. "Look, his gold mane is back."

"Then it's true, not just a faction nor a fiction. A horse

or pony *can* become a unicorn," Alicia said, her voice full of wonder.

"Oh, so much is true." Gundersnap beamed, and from her pocket she took out a handful of the most glorious fat rubies any of them had ever seen. So brilliant was their ruby-red light that it caught all of them in its radiance. But the most radiant of all was Princess Gundersnap, who was as beautiful as any princess in the entire camp of princesses.

That evening when the clock began to chime midnight, the four princesses made their way up the winding staircase of the hidden turret. They took up their needles and thread and began to stitch.

"You should do these last stitches," Princess Alicia said, nodding toward the short little horn that grew out of the creature in the tapestry. Gundersnap stepped up with her needle and thread. She began to stitch. Now at last it was all so clear as she began to stitch the final images of two unicorns flying through a starry night. One was ridden by a princess—a radiant, lovely princess.

Outside summer had slipped back to spring. It was almost as if the princesses could hear the new grass pushing up. And tomorrow there would be daffodils, and Gundersnap would go to a place in the meadow where she knew the sweetest clover grew to feed her dear Menschmik.

"So I guess the tapestry is finished, the story told," Gundersnap said as she broke off the thread from her last stitch.

Really? thought Princess Kristen. The princess from the Realm of Rolm narrowed her eyes. In another part of the tapestry, some pale-green stitches looked the same color as the water in the lake where the campers swam, but it was as if the stitches had broken in the lake's center and the head of something very strange was rising from the waves. It was rather frightening. And were there flames coming from its mouth? Was it some sort of dragon, a water dragon? Kristen squinted harder.

The tapestry was not finished! And this mystery was hers to solve, Kristen's, the princess from the Isles of the Salt Tears in the Realm of Rolm. A dragon, though? There hadn't been dragons for centuries. And here at Camp Princess? Maybe. She'd have to send for armor. The lightweight, waterproof, no-rust chain mail. She'd seen the perfect set in the *Knights and Squires Survival Catalogue*. And would her dad lend her his sword? Could she pray for a sword? It didn't seem quite right . . . but maybe. Yes, by Saint Michael, patron saint of war, she could. If there was a patron saint, it was okay to pray—right?

Whatever!